GERALDINE MOORKENS BYRNE

# The Kimberly Killing Revised

First edition

This book was professionally typeset on Reedsy.
Find out more at reedsy.com

# Contents

# Chapter 1

To the Real Old Bats
They Know Who They Are

# Preface

Welcome to the world of Bramble Lane, a quiet wee road off a leafy Dublin Suburb. It's only a small community, a crescent of artisan cottages from the late eighteen hundreds, and you can find several real examples scattered throughout the greater Dublin area. Once these were rural villages, swallowed up ruthlessly by the city as it swelled outwards across the county of Dublin. Merrion is the name of a real suburb, one in which I used to live, but I have taken huge liberties with its location and description. However like Bramble Lane, the Merrion of my book echoes other real suburbs.

All of the folk traditions and magical beliefs mentioned are based on real Irish lore. If you are interested, there's a section at the end of the book that explains them. As a nation we believe in many "piseógs" or folk beliefs. They range from good luck charms to divination, and the traditional practitioner was a "Wise woman," or Bean Feasa in Irish. Another word is "Draoi" (Irish word roughly translating as magic or magic user.)

The events recounted as part of Kimberly Cottage's history are based on real stories, the treatment many women experienced in the nineteen hundreds and into modern times.

The residents of Bramble Lane love their gardens and their

cottages; they reflect the individuality of the residents. I have included a map so you can visualize the layout of the cottages.

# Acknowledgement

Grateful thanks are owed as usual to my husband Mark for his endless patience in reading and providing feedback and my children for being the funny, supportive, cheerleaders that they are. Similarly, I owe my thanks to all at PPP Publishing; to the very kind beta reading team who provided invaluable feedback; and to the friends who wholeheartedly embraced the fun, and magic, of Bramble Lane.

Many thanks as well to the real Old Bats who constantly remind me that growing old is no excuse not to cause trouble.

# Map of Bramble Lane

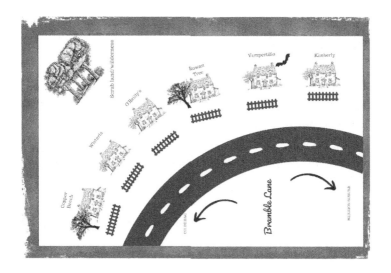

# Chapter 1

Eve Caulton waited until the moving van, carrying the two burly men who had unpacked all her cases and boxes, pulled out of the driveway. Then she quietly shut the door and did a happy dance.

She touched the walls, hugged the curtains and blew kisses to the furniture, before sinking into her new sofa and laughing happily. It was a dream come true, she told herself, and nothing short of miraculous, to have bought this small but lovely house in Dublin city . Doubly so, at a time when house prices were sky high and houses in short supply. Even now she had to pinch herself to know it was real. A perfect little house, in a quiet suburb, at a reasonable price. It was "as rare as hen's teeth," as her Granny would have said.

Eve had looked everywhere in the city. She had tried every area, waited outside properties for hours just to be told someone else had offered a few thousand above her budget. As a semi-retired art teacher slash artist, her budget wasn't tremendously high even with half the sale of her old home. She had shed many a tear putting her lovely four bed-roomed semi-detached up for sale but at least it had given her something to start over with. The market was brutal in Dublin, even with cash to buy.

When she had seen the advertisement for Kimberly Cottage

in the real estate agent's window, she hadn't held out much hope. Neither had the smug young man who took her details and arranged a viewing.

"We expect this one to be snapped up," he warned. "It's under-valued in my personal opinion. The owner should have accepted our professional opinion – but no matter. Once it goes to auction, it will fetch a good price."

Her heart sank. If it went to auction, with the Irish house market the way it was, it would be out of her reach. But she couldn't resist going to look at it, anyway. "You're only tormenting yourself, Eve."

Her mother couldn't understand why she wanted to move out. Why not stay home with her Mam, all the home comforts and no mortgage to pay off? Eve had smiled, not wanting to hurt her mother's feelings but at fifty years of age, living at home with her mother and bachelor brother, Conor, didn't appeal. Not when she had lived in her own house, with her lovely bits and pieces...but no point dwelling on that now. Peter had left, and that life was over now. She had two grown children, Mairead the eldest and Liam the youngest. Mairead worked in marine biology, living on the Renvyle Peninsula in Galway. Liam was doing well in what Eve thought of as "computers," but was aware it was something very techie and high-faluting. She didn't have to worry about them. She had her share of the family home; sold off as soon as Liam had turned eighteen, as soon as Irish law would permit. Peter needed the money for his second wife, the glamourous Liza. She had her work as a lecturer in the local Adult Education centre, and her real passion, her art. Things could be worse.

If Conor had moved out, or even now, shown any signs of wanting to live a different life, it would change things. Eve

7

would have stayed with her mother and let him off. But Conor was a gentle soul, happy in his routine and had been horrified at the suggestion.

"It's not for me, Eve," he had said firmly. "I appreciate it, I do. But I haven't stayed here in some mad sacrifice, you know. It was always what I wanted. It suits me. I've my pals, we have a nice social life, and believe it or not, Mam and I are perfectly happy. We rub along nicely."

Conscience salved, Eve had started her house search on a wave of optimism. But house hunting in Dublin was a different game from when she was first married. Prices had soared and there were more people looking than there were houses to buy. Renting was difficult, buying was near impossible. She was about to accept defeat and wait until things calmed down when she spotted Kimberly Cottage.

"*This charming period cottage is one of a row of artisan dwellings, situated in a secluded laneway in the heart of Merrion, one of Dublin's most sought after suburban areas.*" The blurb was enticing.

She read the prospectus again, trying to conjure up memories. "I used to know that area when I was in University," Back when she and Peter Dunne were young and in love and had planned great careers together. He as an architect and she as an artist, maybe a writer too. "It's a lovely spot."

"It's very popular," Craig the estate agent said flatly. "Most houses there are at least seven hundred and fifty thousand. Of course, the cottages are small so they won't fetch anything like that but still..." He let the sentence hang in the air to show Eve how very unlikely it was someone like her could afford it. "It's more suited to a young, professional couple."

Eve smiled. "Let's go look, anyway," she replied. "No harm

in looking."

Craig sighed and she was sure he rolled his eyes at her as he fetched the keys to the cottage. She could sense the irritation coming off him in waves, which made her even more determined to go look at the place. Cheeky young pup! Maybe it would end up being out of her price range but he could be a bit nicer about it.

Driving to Kimberly Cottage only took ten minutes in the end. They turned onto a broad, tree-lined avenue, with large houses behind wrought iron gates. It was mid September and Autumn was already touching the trees with russet, gold and orange. She could imagine walking through piles of crunchy leaves on some crisp morning. There was a row of well-kept shops - a small mini market, a pharmacy and an Italian fish 'n' chip takeaway. The very modern, very expensive shopping centre called the Merrion Complex could just be seen from the corner. The next turn was onto Bramble Lane, where Kimberly cottage was to found. The cottage was first in a row of detached dwellings, each with a small front garden and a larger back plot; they were originally quite small buildings, but many had dormer conversions and extensions out the back, including Kimberly. Eve glanced again at the brochure. Two decent sized bedrooms upstairs, one en suite and downstairs a kitchen, sitting room, bathroom and small study,

Craig parked in the driveway and Eve stepped out into the garden. Her heart soared. The front garden even in early autumn was a riot of colour, with chrysanthemums and dahlias, echinaceas and calla lilies. It had the charm of a wildflower meadow, but it was obviously a labour of love, created by someone who actually knew what they were doing. In her old house, Peter had insisted on landscape gardeners taking care of everything. He hated flowers, which in retrospect should have been a red flag. Their gardens were tasteful, minimalist and filled with shrubs and low maintenance ground cover. Kimberly Cottage was a fairy-tale garden, Eve thought. And there was even a hoop of climbing roses still blooming, arching over the front door. Mixed in with the roses was a plant she was reasonably sure was wisteria, meaning it would have flowers from early spring.

She half expected the interior to be a disappointment compared to her first impressions of the garden but instead, it surprised a gasp of delight from her. The door opened onto a tiny lobby, with the stairs to the first floor directly in front of her and to the left, a door leading into a light, airy sitting room. Another door led from this room into the kitchen, which was neatly organized making the most of every nook and cranny for storage, with room for one quite large table, and six chair. A back door opened onto a spacious garden, with patio, and a lawn dotted with daisies and forget-me-nots, bordered by large raised flowerbeds. Or vegetable beds, Eve thought longingly. Herbs too. She followed Craig up stairs to two large bedrooms, front-facing and flooded with early afternoon light.

"It's perfect," she said. "I can see why you think it'll go quickly."

"Yes, I did say," Craig sniffed. "Well, you wanted to see it and you have."

Eve tried not to show her annoyance. She wasn't one of those middle-aged women who thought all young people were rude. Her own kids and their friends were very polite. Most young people were polite and she admired how much they cared about issues. But there were some like Craig who thought older women in particular were beneath their notice. At fifty, Eve certainly didn't feel old - her own mother was hale and hearty at eighty-six - but she supposed to Craig, she was a dinosaur.

Ah well. It wasn't like she had much hope of buying it anyway. She took one last longing look out the kitchen window and blushed as she realized she was under close scrutiny. An older woman, mid seventies at a guess, was peering over the back wall from the next house. She stared at Eve, quite openly, and when Eve went to turn away, the old woman waved her hand imperiously and called out, "Hello! You there!"

Craig stiffened beside her. "Oh no." "Who is that?" Eve asked.

"It's Mrs Moriarty. The next door neighbour. I knew this would happen." He muttered the last bit under his breath. "Old Bat."

Eve frowned at him. "That's very rude, Craig."

It was his turn to blush. "Oh. Sorry. But she's very difficult. We need to go, before she catches us on the doorstep."

He moved to the door as he spoke, wrenched it open and then gave a squeal of fright as Mrs Moriarty popped up. She was a tall, spare woman, dark hair twisted into a neat bun and easily Eve's height. Seeing her up close, Eve revised her estimate of her age to early eighties, but she was well preserved for her age. She certainly had to be nimble, to have moved from the back garden to the front so quickly. The woman looked around with an air of authority, ignoring the young real estate agent. Her eye lit on Eve, standing in the middle of the living room, and her rather stern face relaxed into a smile.

"You're interested in the cottage?"

Eve nodded. "Well, yes. Although I'm afraid it'll be beyond my price range."

"Hmm. We'll see about that. You look familiar, would I know

you?"

Not for the first time, Eve had an internal chuckle at the Irish turn of phrase. We're a great people for asking unreasonable things in an equally unreasonable way, she thought.

"I don't know," She smiled. "I'm not famous or anything. Maybe I just remind you of someone."

Mrs Moriarty nodded briskly. "That's probably it. Do you like the place?"

"I love it," Eve admitted. "It's just perfect."

"Have you children?" "Yes. Two. But they're grown up now."

"Ah. Good. They won't be wrecking the place, is what I mean."

"They wouldn't have done that even as little kids," Evelyn pointed out, "They're good kids, always were."

"So you say. But I suppose that's reasonable enough. Any pets?"

"Not yet!" Eve laughed and added, "I need a house before I worry about getting a pet."

"I'm not one for them myself," Mrs Moriarty replied. "But still, a dog makes a good companion. Or a hedgehog. We could do with keeping the garden pests down."

"Okay." She could see Craig who had slipped past the old woman and was frantically waving at her from the driveway. "Well, it was nice to meet you. I'll have to go now."

She stepped past the neighbour who nodded but shot out one bony hand and closed on her wrist. Her grip was stronger than expected from an older lady. "Put in an offer, Dear." Mrs. Moriarty fixed her dark blue eyes on Eve's green ones and peered at her earnestly. "Put in a fair offer. You never know."

Eve was quiet all the way back to the agency, where her own

car was parked. Craig made small talk, but in an absent kind of way. He was already thinking of his next appointment. When she got into her car, Eve turned the afternoon over and over in her head. Kimberly Cottage was so perfect, her heart ached. And the way Mrs. Moriarty had said she recognized her and advised her to bid on it, was like a sign. Making her mind up suddenly, Eve rang the agency number, hoping it wouldn't be Craig who answered.

To her relief a polite female voice said "Murphy, Mullen and Chase, Real Estate. Orla speaking. How may I help you?" and Eve found herself explaining that she wanted to offer on Kimberly Cottage. She named a figure that was just above the asking price, the absolute height of her budget. There was a short pause and Orla replied "That seems fair. I'll pass it on."

"I won't get it," Eve told her mother later that night, "but at least I tried."

"You never know, pet. That which is for you, won't pass you by. I know that, better than most. If I hadn't met your dad, I'd still be stuck in a dirty kip of a place, skivvying for my sisters. If this place is meant for you, it'll be yours. Light a candle."

From most Irish mothers this would have meant light a candle to a saint in a church. From her mother, it could mean that, or it could mean light a candle and meditate or it could mean work a spell to make Kimberly Cottage hers. It was hard to know when your mother was a Bean Feasa, what others outside of Ireland might call a witch, but Irish people called wise women, or people with the sight, or the touch. Eve had it herself to some degree, but life as a suburban mother and working woman had pushed it to one side. Maybe if she wanted Kimberly, it might be time to put some effort into the old ways. Try everything, you might as well, Eve told herself. She was too self conscious to attempt anything more than lighting a candle and wishing hard. Still, her mother would be doing all she could too.

Two days later, Orla from Murphy, Mullen and Chase rang to say her offer had been accepted and could she call by the office? Once the paperwork had been arranged, she had been presented with a double set of front door keys and one back door key, Orla apologizing that the previous owner had mislaid the spare one. Eve didn't care, once she was in residence everything else could be sorted then. And now hardly a fortnight later, the leaves on the Merrion Avenue had turned a shade more colourful, there was fruit on the blackberry bushes that lined Bramble Lane, and she was sitting in the living room of her very own sweet little home.

"This is perfect," Eve thought. "Peace and quiet at last."

# Chapter 2

She had barely begun to unpack some essentials - the kettle, teabags and coffee, cups and plates, her watercolours and other artistic trappings - when a knock at the cottage door made her start. It was a firm knock, almost imperious. She wasn't a bit surprised to open it and find Mrs. Moriarty on the doorstep.

"I won't come in," her neighbour announced. "I just called round to give you this." Eve found a dish pushed into her hands: it was still warm. A smell of chicken, tasty roasted chicken, wafted from it. "It's chicken and herbs, with garden veg. From my own garden, none of that supermarket rubbish. Welcome to Bramble Lane." "Oh wow," Eve managed. "Will you not come in and join me? This smells delicious..." Her stomach growled in agreement.

"No, you settle yourself in. I'll call in again tomorrow. By the way, I remembered where I know you from."

There was an air of sly amusement about the way she said it. She obviously wanted Eve to ask her about it, and seeing as she had kindly provided dinner, Eve obliged.

"Oh, have we met before? I'm so sorry, I can't remember but I'd love to know."

A grin appeared on the old woman's face, making her look

less forbidding and younger. "I know your mother. You're Niamh Caulton's girl."

Eve stared. "I am. But...how on earth did you make the connection?"

Niamh Caulton was a small bird of a woman, whereas Eve took after her father's people. The Caultons were a tall, well built, handsome people, and nothing like the dainty Boyds, her mother's family. For someone to say she looked like her mother struck her as unlikely. She saw a twinkle in Mrs. Moriarty's eye and the penny dropped. "Oh."

"Yes, dear. I knew the moment I saw you. It took a while to place you, but there are only so many of us around. And you have your mother's eyes, the colour if not the shape, and you have her mannerisms. Your voice too."

"Well," Eve said weakly, "Isn't it some coincidence, me moving in here next door to you." What were the odds? she asked herself.

"Coincidence? Oh, my dear. My eldest granddaughter, Orla, works at Murphy, Mullen and Chase. I think you've met her?" The woman chuckled at Eve's face. "Don't look so shocked, pet. We help our own. Especially around here. Bramble Lane is a very special place, can't have just anyone moving in."

She gave one last smug nod and trotted off briskly down the garden path, leaving Eve standing rather foolishly on her doorstep. It took Eve a minute to process things, then she laughed and shrugged. "I suppose Mam is right," she thought, "That which is for you, won't pass you by. If an old crony of Mam's fancied helping me get the place, I'm not arguing." So many things in Ireland operated on the Old Boy's Network, why not take advantage of the Old Bat Network! Not that she would dare call either Mrs. Moriarty or her mother an old bat to her face. She pulled back the foil covering the dish of chicken and her mouth watered. Dinner break, then back to unpacking.

The next bang on the door came just as she finished her meal. A sharp rap, followed quickly by another rap. Impatient, Eve thought. She opened the door cautiously to find a red-faced man, middle aged but slim, dressed in what she thought of as expensive work out gear. Although people seemed to wear the same gear to go shopping or to the pub these days. The man on her doorstep looked as if he'd been jogging, but possibly he was just angry.

"Is that your car?" He snapped before she could speak.

Eve glanced at her car, parked in her driveway.

"It is." "Are you going to be parking it there?"

"I am."

He glowered at her. "This is most inconvenient."

"I do apologize," Eve replied, "But it *is* my car, in my own driveway, on my own property."

"I never said it wasn't!" he replied with an outraged expression. "But no one informed me that the new tenants would be using the driveway."

"I'm not a tenant," remarked Eve, beginning to wonder if the man was a trifle unhinged.

"What?"

"I am the new owner," she elaborated.

He stared at her, his face now an alarming shade of puce. "What are you talking about?" he asked rudely. "Owner? You mean it's been sold already?"

"Yes." Eve drew herself up to her full height and looked at him with all the dignity she could muster. "And who are you? What business is it of yours where I park?"

He puffed out his chest and replied, "I'm head of the local

neighbourhood watch, that's who."

"I was a volunteer safety monitor in my old job," Eve said cheerfully. "Neither explains why you're asking me such personal questions. Now, let's say we start over. My name is Eve Caulton and I've just bought Kimberly Cottage. I'll be living here, and using my driveway, for the foreseeable future."

Her visitor pursed his lips. "I can't believe Maud Williams sold this house to you."

Maud Williams, the previous owner of the cottage, was in a nursing home from what Orla Moriarty had told her. She had probably gone into one to get away from this bully, Eve thought. But she didn't want to start off on bad terms with a neighbour, so she forced a smile and said politely, "I assure you, Mrs. Williams certainly did. Did you not notice the For Sale sign being taken down?"

"I've been away these last two weeks. Well, I'm absolutely shocked at her. She knew other people were interested. If she wanted a quick sale, she should have spoken to me."

He was silent for a moment, then in a sudden change of approach, smiled ingratiatingly. "Well, well, that's not your fault, I suppose. I'm sorry I was a bit abrupt, but it's been a shock. Mrs. Williams doesn't drive and she allowed my wife park her car in the driveway, you see. It's...well, not to be coy, it's rather an expensive car and shouldn't be parked out on the road. Only room for one car in each driveway, so we relied on parking here." He stared at Eve's car, a modest 4-year-old Honda Civic. "Your car would be grand if you parked on the street. Sure, no one would break into that old yoke. It would make a lot more sense if you parked out and let my Frances park here..."

Eve gave a short laugh. "Eh, no. I like my car where it is,

thanks. It might not be as expensive as yours, or your wife's but it's all I've got. So I will not be parking on the street, thank you very much. Now, Mister...?"

"Mister O'Reilly," He snapped.

"Mr. O'Reilly. Thank you for calling around, but I need to get back to unpacking now. Bye."

She shut the door firmly and leaned against it, torn between laughter and outrage. What a horrible, entitled man. She wondered what his wife was like - either a bully like him, or a saint to put up with him. Eve peeked out the window to check whether Mr. O'Reilly had left yet. She was just in time to catch him shaking a fist at her closed door, before stomping away.

It was an unpleasant encounter, but the outrageous nature of his demands made it hard to take him seriously. She made a mental note to ask Mrs. Moriarty about him and then resolutely pushed it aside and went back to the task at hand.

It was almost dark when she decided she had done enough, the nights closing in around seven now that it was late September. She was tired, her back ached and she was sick of unpacking but there was a sense of satisfaction in a job well done. The worst of it was over, and although there were still a few crates left, they were mainly books, waiting to be placed on the built in shelves that lined an entire wall of the sitting room. Maud Williams had obviously been a reader, like Eve. Tomorrow she would arrange her bookshelves, a task she was looking forward to. A lot of her books had been in storage too long, getting them on shelves would be like a reunion with old friends.

To one side of the living room, she had already set up her easel, work table and a handy shelf she filled with an assortment of paints, medium and brushes in neat holders. The light in the mornings would be excellent, and she suspected even in the afternoon there would be a decent quality of natural light to rely on. It was smaller than her studio in the old house but at least it was a space dedicated to her art again. She was very much a fan of painting "en Plein air," out in natural light so she would manage in this small area when she needed to. It was, she reminded herself, her own space in her own home. That made up for a lot.

"First night," Eve thought. It wasn't her old home, which made it bittersweet. Whatever had gone wrong in their marriage, she and Peter had made a gracious and attractive home together. But this was all hers, and she felt at home for the first time in years. By the time she had made up a bed, with freshly aired linen and her favourite duvet set, and scoffed a rough and ready supper she was ready for bed. In the coming week, she would get a television in, and WiFi, too. But she could live without technology for a while, quite happily.

It was easy to fall asleep, sheer physical exhaustion taking over. She slept deeply until the early hours of the morning, waking suddenly to a dark room with just a shaft of moonlight peeking through the curtains. Eve lay quietly, trying to figure out what had wakened her. She let the sounds of the old house wash over her, every creaking sigh of the old place as it settled. It was quite chilly, she thought sleepily. Must set the central heating tomorrow. Maybe light a fire in the living room fireplace, help air the place out. No trace of damp anywhere though, which was a good thing. Her eyes had almost closed again, when a sound at the window made her sit upright in the bed. It had sounded just like a tap on the window, which was disconcerting when you slept on the first floor. It wouldn't be welcome in the middle of the night on the ground floor either, admittedly. Eve strained her ears, and then sure enough, it happened again. A tap, tap, at the window.

She leapt out of bed, and whisked both curtains back, revealing...a small bat. Eve laughed out loud in relief. A nocturnal visitor, but nothing to be scared of - just a poor wee creature getting a bit disoriented. She looked at it sympathetically, and it hovered for a moment before flying away somewhat unsteadily towards the garden next door. Chuckling at her own fright, Eve clambered back into bed, wrapped herself up firmly in the duvet and went asleep. It had been an interesting first day, was her last fuzzy thought before sleep overtook her. "I must ask Mrs. M about that awful man...."

As she drifted off, there was a rustle in the garden next door, then a slight thud, followed by a quiet but heartfelt "OW!" But Eve was fast asleep by then.

# Chapter 3

True to her word, Mrs. Moriarty called around mid morning, this time clutching a tray of buns. "Elevenses," she said, "I was baking anyway. My grand kids will be around later." She glanced around the sitting room. "It's looking good. I see you're a reader."

Eve smiled at the obvious note of approval. "Yes, I've always been into books." "Like your mother. Have you passed on my regards to her yet?"

"I did, last night. She remembers you well. When she comes over to visit, you must call over."

Mrs. Moriarty permitted herself a smile, obviously pleased to be asked. "I wouldn't mind seeing Niamh Boyd again. We knew each other as girls, you know. I knew her before she married your father, she'll always be a Boyd to me. Lost touch over the years, as you do. But we always got on well."

Eve's mother had said similar when they had chatted the previous evening. Her mother was also pleased that an old crony was living next to her precious daughter. Honestly, even at fifty years of age, her mother still saw her as a fifteen-year-old not fit to be left unsupervised.

The iced buns were as delicious as the previous night's dinner. After her third helping, Eve remembered to ask, "Do you know a Mr. O'Reilly? I don't know his first name, but he has a wife called Frances?"

Mrs. Moriarty executed an eye roll any teenager would be proud of before replying.

"Do I know him? He's the bane of our existence - everyone on Bramble Lane, I mean. He's a middle-aged, spoiled, man-child. Brian O'Reilly, indeed. What did he want?"

"He wanted me to move my car to the street so his wife can park her expensive car in my driveway." Eve grinned at the look on her neighbour's face. "Yeah. You can imagine my reply! Apparently, he had some arrangement with the previous owner." "He bullied Maud Williams into letting his harridan of a wife park there, you mean," Mrs Moriarty said indignantly. "Maud came home one day to find the car in her driveway, and when she asked, he just blustered at her until the poor woman gave in. Tom - that's Thomas MacDonagh, he's two doors down from you next to me, he tried to make Brian O'Reilly see sense but even he had to give up."

"It's not just me, then," Eve was relieved. "I kept wondering why he was so aggressive, I thought I must have done something to annoy him. But I'm not going to allow him or anyone else bully me into a ridiculous arrangement like that."

"Good girl. And no one around here likes the man. He's rude, greedy and a downright nuisance."

"He was very put out that the house was sold. He thought I was renting, and when I put him straight, he was pretty angry."

The older woman chuckled. "He thought he would swoop in and buy it up. That's why Maud asked my Orla to take it on. Gave her exclusive rights. Even at that, she had to fight off the vultures in that office of hers."

"Craig, the young man who showed me the house, he was

dead set on putting me off, now I think of it," Eve mused. "He made me feel like it was pointless even trying. Until you said to give it a go, I had given up any hope of bidding."

"I told Maud about you. She was delighted, a quick sale and to someone who would appreciate the place. If she wasn't so frail, it would have been worth her while hanging on to it, getting the government grant for the nursing home. But she hasn't long left, the poor woman, and she wanted her affairs in order. This was a relief to her. And you'll like it here. This is a lovely little community, despite O'Reilly. You have Tom, he's a widower, retired. He used to have an auction house. A real expert in antiques. Beside him, the O'Reilly house, and then young Margaret Furey. She's a teacher over in St. Malachy's Primary school, lovely girl."

"I know that school," Eve said, "I taught art there. Years ago now, when I was young."

Mrs. Moriarty looked at her over the top of her mug of tea. "Before you were married?" Eve had to admire how the old lady managed to imply so much in so few words.

"Yes. Before Peter and I were married. We're divorced now, of course."

Her neighbour sniffed. "You're better off without. I buried Fintan Moriarty twenty years ago and I'm not saying he wasn't a good husband, for he was. And I'm not saying I don't miss him, because I do. But a woman survives better without a man, than men do without women. Ever seen an auld bachelor my age? They're walking shambles. But a single woman in her eighties will have clubs, friends, hobbies...yes, women don't much need a man."

Eve busied herself with pouring another cup of tea to hide her grin. "I think you might be on to something there, Mrs.

Moriarty."

"Call me Dymphna."

"Dymphna, thank you. But I haven't quite ruled out meeting someone."

It was true, although Eve had never said it out loud before. From the moment they separated, everyone she knew assumed that Peter would naturally marry again, or at least have a girlfriend. But they assumed that her romantic life was dead and buried at fifty, never to be spoken of again.

"Oh by all means," Dymphna Moriarty waved her hand airily, "Sure, why not? Aren't you a decent looking woman with your own means? You're a catch. Just don't go thinking you *need* them, that's all."

"I won't," promised Eve. "So, tell me more about the neighbours. Who lives beside Margaret?" Bramble Lane boasted 6 cottages, all on the one side. Eve counted herself, Dymphna, Tom, the O'Reillys, and Margaret Furey. That left one cottage.

"Ah. Well at the end of the row, you have young Ronan. Ronan Desmond. He's a bit of a dark horse, is that young man."

"Oooh. I like it. A man of mystery. What makes him so intriguing."

Mrs. Moriarty glanced at her. "Would you not be well able to suss him out yourself?"

Eve reddened a little. "I'm not my mother," she replied gruffly. It was a bit of a sensitive issue, always being expected to have her mother's gifts. Dymphna raised an eyebrow in response, and muttered, "Nonsense," but when Eve didn't rise to the bait, she shrugged and continued, "He is perfectly nice and friendly, but after three years living here, no one seems to know much about him. He works odd hours, he avoids any questions about his work, or his personal life. Doesn't seem to have any hobbies. But he seems a decent chap all the same."

"So, everyone sounds nice, except the O'Reillys."

"Oh, yes. It's a very pleasant little community. They're all terribly pleased about you buying Kimberly Cottage, you know. No one wanted Brian O'Reilly buying it, or one of his pals. Can you imagine it? A pair of them on the same road."

Eve shook her head. "No. One of them is quite enough. I've still to meet his wife, and I'm not looking forward to that."

"Hah! Yes, you've a treat ahead of you. Well, my dear, I hope you're settling in well. Maud was a good neighbour, and I hope we can be too." She patted Eve's hand. "Don't be putting yourself down, either. You've a sensitive soul - trust your instincts. Drop back my dishes when you've finished with them." After her visitor left, Eve turned her attention to her books. But as she unpacked, the sun shone into the sitting room, and she could hear birds chirping away. At this point in the year, sunny days were getting rarer. It seemed a pity to sit indoors all day, no matter how much needed to be done.

She made up her mind. A short walk, get to know the area a bit, have a look at the rest of the cottages, then back to putting the books in order. It was warm enough to not need a jacket, all she needed were her keys and phone. With a slightly giddy feeling, as if she was skipping school or a teen sneaking out of the house, she set off. At the end of her driveway, she turned right and walked past Mrs. Moriarty's house - a small brass plaque on the gateway pillars marked it as *Vespertilio Cottage*, and she wondered if that was Dymphna's choice or whether she had inherited the name. Eve couldn't imagine changing the name of Kimberly Cottage, it was too pretty. Her neighbour's cottage had a garden to rival her own, and the house itself was a mix of pleasing pastel colours, including a soft buttercream colour on the walls and a light pink door.

She looked for a nameplate on the next cottage - Rowan Tree House. Sure enough, in the middle of a well cultivated lawn, bordered by neat flower beds, stood a Rowan tree, laden with the usual orange-red berries. Thomas "Tom" MacDonagh had opted for an easy to maintain garden, but the flower beds were colourful, and while his cottage had plain white walls, the windows and door were painted a bright, cheerful red. She thought she would like Tom, going by his home.

Next was the O'Reilly's house. Like the others, it had a name plate but this one said, in neat script engraved on a shiny gold background, "The O'Reilly Residence." Eve stuck her tongue out at it and muttered, "Typical. Pure notions." The worst thing in Ireland was to be accused of notions, a mixture of being stuck up and pretentious. Notions above your station. Notions of grandeur. The O'Reilly's were definitely aiming for urban chic rather than charming cottage vibes. The garden here was all lawn, bordered by ornate quartz blocks and a carefully paved driveway. The house itself was painted white, with a brown door inlaid with stained glass. "Plain. And a bit boring." Eve decided.

She strolled on and examined Margaret Furey's place. "Wisteria Cottage," she read the neat silver plate on the driveway pillar. "I like that." And the garden didn't disappoint. A low border of green shrubs surrounded what she could only describe as a wildflower meadow. It was not at its best in Autumn but her artist's eye appreciated the potential for Spring and Summer - she would love to paint it in full bloom. A little bench sat against the wall under the windows, hanging baskets on brackets bloomed either side of the front door. A sweet little arrangement of garden ornaments comprised of hedgehogs, birds, puppies in shoes decorated one side of the driveway. There was an excellent showing of Chrysanthemums and a purple flower which she didn't recognize was coming into bloom. It promised to be eye-catching.

"Love it," was Eve's verdict. She hurried on to the last cottage and looked for a name. "Copper Beech Cottage." And yes, there it was - a Copper Beech tree in the middle of another well-kept lawn. This garden was rather plain compared to the others, but a water feature added a touch of whimsy. A spurt of water rose from a pipe and splashed on to two stone otters, playing in the water. It struck her as interesting: maybe Ronan Desmond did have a hobby - in her opinion, people who liked otters and water might like fishing.

The afternoon had turned a little cloudy. Time to get back to work, but she didn't mind now. The little excursion had done the trick, and seeing the individual results her neighbours had made of identical cottages and gardens had caught her imagination. Her mind deep in a mixture of garden planning and ideas for a painting, she fished her house keys out of her pocket. As she went to put the Yale key in the lock, to her surprise the door swung open.

"Eve! You absolute numpty," she chastised herself. "Imagine going out and not checking the door was properly locked." She had heard it click shut, but she supposed an old door must have its vagaries. Still grumbling to herself she turned into the sitting room and froze in shock.

The scene that met her eyes was one of horror. A young woman, her face ashen and her hands gripped together until the knuckles were white, was standing in the centre of the room. At her feet, lying face down over a pile of Eve's precious books was a familiar figure. It looked like her neighbour, Brian O'Reilly, and a knife was buried in his back up to the hilt.

Eve couldn't even scream. Her throat seemed to close in and all that could escape was a high-pitched squeak. It was enough to alert the woman, who turned sharply.

"Oh!" she said, "Please, help me."

Eve's eyes fixed on the prone body and the woman flinched, cowering back.

"Oh no, no! I didn't do it. I swear, it wasn't me."

All Eve could do was stand and stare, unable to speak or escape.

# Chapter 4

A movement behind her made her jump, breaking the paralysis. Spinning around, she found herself looking at a pleasant-faced man, grey haired but quite youthful looking, with a pair of friendly brown eyes.

"Are you okay?" He indicated the open door. "I was passing and - " His attention was caught by the scene in front of her, and he gasped. "Good god, what's happened?"

"It wasn't me, Tom," the woman sobbed. "I didn't do it."

The man looked from her to the corpse, but his face remained neutral.

"Of course not, Margaret. Come away now, like a good woman. Come on out. We'll call the police." He looked anxiously at Eve. "Come out, we'll ring for help."

She followed him out into the garden, shivering at the cold breeze that had whipped up. The young woman, Margaret, was hardly able to stand. The newcomer, Tom, held her up with one hand and tried to manage his mobile phone with the other. Watching him struggle, Eve snapped back into herself. "Here, I'll ring," she dialled 999 and asked for the Gardaí. The operator snapped "What's the nature of your emergency?"

"A man is dead," Eve replied flatly.

"Are you sure you don't require the Ambulance service? The

Gardaí are for when it's a crime."

"I'm fairly sure it's a crime," Eve replied. "There's a dagger sticking out of his back."

"Oh. Hang on the line then, I'll put you through." "Gardaí," A voice drawled. "What's the nature of your..."

"Death," Evelyn cut across him firmly. There was a marked lack of urgency about the emergency phone service, in her opinion. "There's a dead man, in my living room. I came home to find him there. And a woman. I need the Gardaí, please."

"Right. I'll get a car out to you now, just give me the address. I'll send an ambulance too. You never know."

"I'm fairly sure," Eve muttered.

"And do you know the victim?"

"Yes. Well, not exactly. It's a neighbour. I only met him the once."

"Ah. And this woman...the one who was also there?"

Eve glanced at Margaret, whom she assumed was Margaret Furey from Wisteria Cottage. She looked pathetic. Sobbing had given way to a full-blown attack of hysterics.

"Look, I don't know anything, I've just moved in here and I barely know my own address. Please, how long will it be until the officers arrive?"

As if in answer to her question, sirens broke the afternoon peace and a squad car turned onto Bramble Lane, followed by an unmarked car with a siren attached to the roof. They pulled up outside Kimberly Cottage, and two uniformed officers hopped out from the squad car. Behind them, two plainclothes men exited the unmarked car; the detectives, Eve presumed. One was older, a tough looking individual who strode purposefully towards them. The other was younger, a tall dark-haired man who looked worried. He hesitated slightly before following his colleague. Eve watched as he stared at Tom, Margaret and finally Eve herself, in turn.

"Tom. Margaret," he said quietly. "What's going on?"

"Ronan?" Tom stared at the detective. "Detective Desmond at the moment, I'm afraid."

Eve started. So, this was the enigmatic Ronan Desmond. No wonder he didn't talk about work, especially to the friendly but nosy neighbours. And what a shock for the young man, to hear his own road being called out by the emergency dispatcher! She wondered where Dymphna Moriarty was - surely she wouldn't miss a commotion next door for anything. She stepped forward and greeted Detective Desmond.

"We haven't met yet, Detective. But I'm your new neighbour. My name is Eve Caulton. I've just moved into Kimberly Cottage."

He nodded. "I heard we had a new resident. This is Detective Cullen, Garda Maguire and Garda Hickey. We need to examine the scene, so if you could just wait here a moment..."

At a nod from Detective Cullen, the uniformed officers entered the house. There was a solemn silence in the garden. Eve half expected them to come out laughing, saying that Brian had just slipped and was okay. That she had imagined the knife...

Garda Maguire reappeared and shook her head. "Dead, sir. Knife wound."

Both detectives sighed.

"Right." Ronan Desmond turned to Detective Cullen.

"I'll take inside," Cullen responded to the unspoken query. "You take statements. Maguire, ring it in."

Ronan turned to Tom MacDonagh. "Want to start off, Tom? What happened here?"

Tom shook his head. "I only arrived at the last moment,

Ronan - I mean, Detective. Margaret and this lady -" he nodded at Eve - "were on the scene first."

They all looked expectantly at Eve.

"I was out for a walk," she said simply. "I came home to find the door slightly ajar. At first, I thought it was burglars, then I assumed I must have forgotten to close it properly. When I stepped inside, I saw this lady standing there, with Brian O'Reilly lying on the floor...well, lying over a pile of books to be accurate. He was face down with what looked like a long handled knife sticking out of his back. I didn't recognize it, by the way. I'm sure it wasn't one of mine. Anyway, that's when Mr. MacDonagh there arrived. Sorry," She added "I'm assuming you're Tom MacDonagh."

"That's me, all right."

"Thank you, Ms. Caulton. That was a very helpful, succinct account." Detective Desmond made some notes in a small, black covered, hard-back notebook. Then he looked at the weeping young woman, still clinging to Tom.

"Margaret?" Eve noticed his tone softened as he addressed the unfortunate teacher. "Are you able to tell me what happened?"

Margaret Furey lifted scared eyes to the detective but seemed reassured by his attitude of kindly interest. For the first time since Eve discovered her in the living room, some faint colour returned to her cheeks and with a deep breath she managed to stop crying.

"I- I was passing by," She sounded unconvincing, Eve thought. "I noticed the door was open, and I knew we had a new resident, so I stuck my head in to say hi. There was no answer so I wondered if she was home, or if something was wrong. I'm sorry, I know it seems rude, but I just came on in.

Um, that's about it. I saw Brian lying there and - and I went to see if he was...well, if he was alive. And then Ms. Caulton came home, and I thought, I realized, it must look awful. But I swear, it wasn't me. I found him like that!"

"She's telling the truth about that, I think" Eve thought, "But the bit about seeing the door open...no. I don't believe that for a minute."

It had been hard to see the door was open up close, never mind from the pathway. And if you stuck your head in and got no reply, you might step in further but you would hardly carefully close the door over behind you.

As if he read her thoughts, Ronan wandered over to the door and pushed it open carefully, using his elbow. The door moved, and then stayed open. It didn't swing back to even half-closed. He raised an eyebrow but made no remark on it. Margaret didn't seem to notice the significance, but Tom cast a worried look at them both.

"Did you see Brian go inside?" the detective asked.

"No!" It sounded to Eve as if Margaret replied a shade too quickly. She pitied the woman, and she couldn't imagine that she was a murderer but she was fairly sure they weren't getting the whole truth. It was also clear that Margaret was desperate for Ronan to think well of her. She looked at him pathetically and repeated "It wasn't me."

"Of course, it wasn't," Tom said. "Nobody thinks that, not for a moment." He looked at Eve and Ronan who both suddenly found something of interest to look at that wasn't Margaret Furey. It was an awkward moment, broken at last by the sound of a car drawing up. As one, they turned to see what was happening. A blue family saloon car had parked across the driveway of the house next door; there were several kids in the back and a dark-haired woman in the driver's seat. The passenger door opened and out stepped Mrs. Moriarty. She was smiling- obviously her grandchildren and daughter had taken her out for the afternoon. The smile faded as she took in the Garda squad car, and the group of neighbours.

"Eve? Margaret?"

Eve raised a hand in greeting. Both Tom and Ronan looked relieved. Margaret was still too upset for Eve to tell what she was feeling. Dymphna strode up the drive, her long black woollen coat flapping behind her, a bit like a bat Eve thought guiltily but a *nice* bat. "What's going on?"

"It's Brian," Tom replied soberly. "Brian O'Reilly. He's...well, he's dead."

"Oh my God!"

"He was killed," Tom continued, looking anxiously from Margaret to Dymphna. "Um, it's been quite a shock all round. Poor Margaret here found him, and then Eve found her and now we have the cops."

A valiant attempt to explain, Eve felt but not terribly success-ful. She caught her next-door neighbour's eye and explained quietly, "I was out for a walk and came home to find Brian in my living room, dead. He'd been stabbed, in the back, and Margaret was there. She says she noticed the door open and came in to see if everything was okay."

Dymphna shot a sharp glance in Margaret's direction before saying, in a carefully neutral voice, "Oh dear. What a terrible experience." She turned on her heel, walked briskly down the drive and had a hurried consultation with the woman Eve assumed was her daughter. Then, as the car drove away amid shouts of "Love you, Granny!" she returned to Eve and her companions, saying "This is ridiculous, standing around on

35

the doorstep. Come into mine, and we'll have a nice cup of tea. Margaret is clearly in shock, she can hardly stand. Come on now!"

# Chapter 5

To Eve's surprise, both Tom and the detective followed meekly, ushering Margaret between them. She hurried after them, suddenly anxious not to be left alone.

"I'm in shock too," she thought somewhat bitterly, "But no one seems terribly concerned about that." She wondered if the roles were reversed and the pretty young teacher had found the middle aged Eve standing over the corpse of their annoying neighbour, would there be tea and chocolate biscuits...

"And how are you?" Tom MacDonagh pulled up an armchair for Eve and hovered solicitously as she took a seat. "I'm so terribly sorry, what a rotten start to your life in your new home. And here we've all been fussing over Margaret, and you've been the one so calm, and brave." Eve's cheeks burned quite red in response.

"Oh. No, no I'm not brave. I mean, obviously it's been a shock but -" She caught a glimpse of Dymphna Moriarty's face, eyebrow raised and a wry twist of the lips, and blushed even deeper. "I mean, thank you."

"Tea, for everyone? Ronan, do you take tea or coffee?"

"Tea, please, Mrs. Moriarty," the detective replied. Eve noticed there was no "Call me Detective Desmond" when he was speaking to Dymphna. The older lady seemed to command a lot of respect. She bustled around, and in no time at all a tray of mugs with a plate of biscuits appeared, followed by another plate of homemade buns.

"Margaret, drink that tea. It has a dollop of sugar in it for shock. And eat a biscuit, there's a good girl." She handed Eve a cup of coffee, also sweetened, without any comment.

"Now. What on earth happened this afternoon?" Between them they explained. Eve found herself watching both Margaret and the young Detective. Margaret's story remained the same, and she saw Ronan Desmond frown anxiously. She also watched Tom MacDonagh. The older man seemed so kind, she thought. A good-looking chap too, not that it mattered. She liked the way he had helped without trying to insert himself into the story. He had recounted his role without embellishment.

Mrs. Moriarty was very solemn once she heard all the details. "How terrible. Margaret, please, do stop telling us it wasn't you. I doubt a person in this room thinks you murdered Brian. Which leaves us with several questions - who did murder him, why did they do it and what was Brian doing in Eve's living room?"

Four pairs of eyes swiveled in Eve's direction.

"I have absolutely no idea!" She protested. "Had you met the deceased, Ms. Caulton?" Ronan had morphed back into the professional Detective. "Eve, please. And yes, I met him briefly. He called to complain that I was parking in my own driveway. Apparently, his wife had an arrangement with Maud Williams to park there. He also let slip that he had wanted to buy Kimberly Cottage and was quite annoyed that Mrs. Williams had sold it."

"Did you row with him?" he was scribbling furiously in his notebook.

"No. I was perfectly polite, and he was..." Eve trailed off. She had been brought up never to speak ill of the dead, especially when the corpse was still cooling.

"He was his usual self, from the sound of it," Tom MacDonagh interjected. A frown from the detective silenced him, but Eve seized on the description.

"Exactly! Not that I knew him, but from what everyone has said, he was just being himself. I told Dymphna about it, didn't I? But then to be honest, I forgot about it. It was impossible to take seriously."

"Okay. So, you have no explanation for why he would be in your house, then?"

"No!"

"And no idea why he would be murdered in your house? Okay. You say you were taking a walk at the time of the incident? Where exactly did you go?" "The length of the road and back, I just wanted to see the other cottages and get a feel for the place." Eve didn't like the way this was going. While Margaret had been protesting her innocence, it had never occurred to Eve she might be a suspect herself. "I was out just under half an hour, I'd say. I had a lot of unpacking still to do, but it was a nice afternoon earlier."

She waited while the detective scribbled down some more notes, then added, "What happens now?"

"Ah. Well, the pathologist will be here soon, but it will take time to examine the body and process the scene. I'm afraid it will be tomorrow before you can get access."

"You'll stay here," Mrs. Moriarty said firmly. "I'm sure they'll let you get some nightclothes and toiletries." It was a statement, almost an instruction. "I'm sure that can be arranged. I have to get back to it, but I'll send Hickey or Maguire

39

around when we're able to let you collect stuff. In the morning we'll ask you all to the station to make formal statements." He hesitated before adding pointedly, "You might want to bring a solicitor, it's advisable."

No one said anything but the atmosphere in the room changed slightly.

"Ms. Caulton, are you certain you didn't recognize the knife?"

"No, definitely not. I don't have anything like that – all I saw was the handle, but it was much longer that anything I use."

He nodded again. "Good, good. Tom, did you recognize it? Margaret? Okay. Then it was definitely brought to the scene, not snatched up. And you have your front door keys, Ms Caulton? Good. Who has spare keys, other than your own spare set?"

"I have a set," Dymphna produced a set identical to Eve's from a drawer in her living room cabinet. "Here, just the front door keys."

Detective Desmond took a note of this. He asked a few more desultory questions but soon stood to take his leave. "I'm needed next door but thank you all. It's always good to get a clear idea of these things at the scene. I'll be talking to you all tomorrow, I hope." His gaze lingered on Margaret Furey, who went even paler. "If you're all up to it, of course."

When he left the room, the remaining four stared at each other. It was Tom MacDonagh who tactfully broke the awkward moment. "Margaret, I think we should get you home and see about some legal representation. I have a good solicitor, but he does houses and probates. Have you anyone?"

"Only the one I used when buying my house," the young woman replied. "Do I need one? It's a statement, surely I can give it without a lawyer?" "Don't," Eve found herself saying, earnestly. "Please don't. You have no idea, once you're in a room giving a statement, they'll ask all kinds of questions. I've been there. My son had to give a statement once about a fight he witnessed, it was bad enough as a mere bystander. If they decide that you're a person of interest, you will definitely need a legal expert."

"Oh."

"I don't want to worry you, but both you and I are in an awkward position. We should be prepared."

"Of course you need a lawyer, didn't Ronan Desmond tell you so? I suppose we should have guessed he was a garda, it explains a lot." Dymphna sniffed. "He wouldn't answer a direct question if you paid him, and he never let on what he worked at. Typical Garda."

"He's only doing his job," Margaret replied, flushing.

"Of course he is," Dymphna replied, "And if he's doing it in any way properly he or that partner of his will grill you til you don't know your own name. Get a lawyer."

Tom volunteered to walk Margaret home and start the process of tracking down a suitable legal representative for her. Once they'd seen them out, Eve turned helplessly to Dymphna. "I suppose I should start looking for one too. That young man seemed to think it was my fault Brian O'Reilly chose my living room to get himself murdered."

"Well, you and Margaret are the obvious suspects. I can't blame him. And remember, he doesn't know you. Maybe you and Brian were old lovers, or you hated him for some reason buried in your dark past. Maybe you moved here solely to kill him , and he recognized you and confronted you."

"What? I only met the man yesterday..."

41

"Oh, I know. But Ronan can't know that, can he? Don't worry though, I have the perfect woman for the job. Let me just find her number and we'll ring."

Eve waited, turning over the incredible events of the afternoon in her mind. What a start to her new life. She'd have to ring Mairead and Liam, and her mother and Conor too. Imagine them hearing on the news "Murder at Kimberly Cottage." They'd assume she was the victim!

"I have it." Dymphna returned clutching a business card triumphantly. "Jennie Warren and Associates. She's Claudia Warren's daughter. You know Claudia - she's a wonderful woman, runs the Merrion branch of the Irish Women's Brigade. In fact, she's second in command of the whole brigade. Rides horses. Your mother knows her."

A vague memory stirred in Eve's brain, of a plump, jolly woman with a very posh accent and a big laugh. "Blonde, cheerful and always baking something?" she ventured. "That's the one! Her daughter Jennie is a solicitor, and she specializes in criminal law. I know, because Claudia hates her being around criminals all the time. I daresay Jennie would be glad to represent someone who is innocent for a change."

"Oh, so you do think I'm innocent, then!" Eve couldn't resist saying.

"Of course I do, dear. I would hardly let you sleep here if I didn't," Dymphna grinned at her. "Come on, let's ring her. Before Ronan Desmond decides to frame you for murder, to save Margaret."

They both laughed, but Eve didn't feel it was entirely impossible.

# Chapter 6

J ennie Warren turned out to be an impressive woman, younger than Eve by about ten years but hugely confident and knowledgeable. She grasped the situation quickly, told Eve to present herself at the local station when requested but to send for her first, as soon as she knew what time she was to appear.

"I'll pick you up if I can. If you go by yourself, do not under any circumstances agree to be interviewed until I arrive. They have to wait for me, so don't let them tell you any different. From what you've described, I can't foresee too much trouble. There's no relationship between you and the deceased, he entered your house without your knowledge and there was another person at the scene before you. But we won't take any chances."

Eve thanked her and rang off feeling exhausted but reassured. Garda Maguire, a cheerful and efficient young woman with a kindly air, had escorted her around Kimberly Cottage to collect nightclothes and toiletries. Eve took the opportunity to ask what was happening, now the body had been removed.

"We've just informed his wife," Maguire confided, "She was in work, up in the Merrion Complex. She owns a boutique in there, very posh place."

Owns, not works there - Eve noticed that. Frances and Brian must have been comfortable financially to own a shop in the very exclusive centre. And it sounded like she had an alibi.

"We'll have some dinner, and then an early night," Dymphna said, as if she had read Eve's thoughts. Maybe she has, Eve thought. She's like Mam, after all. It was both odd and strangely reassuring. It reminded her of being a teenager, trying to put one over on a mother who was sensitive enough to pick up on the tiniest lie. Growing up in a house where magic was a part of life was great and highly irritating in equal parts.

But whatever other skills Dymphna had, she certainly had a talent for cooking. In record time a hot meal of pork chops, mash and home-grown vegetables appeared on the table, followed by a bowl of bread-and-butter pudding with ice-cream. Eve had thought she wouldn't be able to eat but somehow her stomach bypassed her brain, and she ended up pleasantly full and sleepy. Dymphna showed her upstairs, to a pretty bedroom decorated in a tasteful mix of light yellow walls and flower patterned curtains and duvet. A matching set of mahogany wardrobe, chest of drawers and chair added period charm. It looked as if an Edwardian lady might have snuggled in comfortably, as easily as a modern woman.

"Thank you so much for this," Eve was sincerely grateful. "I couldn't have faced some soulless hotel room, or even my mother's house. She will be worried enough as it is." Ringing her family had been a mix of comfort, as they poured out concern and love, but also guilt as they were all so worried and anxious for her. Mairead in particular had wanted to come all the way from Galway and get her mother, saying, "You can't possibly live there now, not after this!" Eve had glossed over it, but she was asking herself the same question. Would Kimberly

Cottage ever feel like home now?

"Sleep on it," Dymphna seemed to know once again what Eve was thinking. "Get as much rest as you can." Exhaustion helped her fall asleep and for several hours she slept deeply. It was a slight noise that woke her, a muffled banging. There was moonlight, and the sky was now clear but the bedside clock showed three a.m. She groaned and turned over, determined to get some sleep when another noise disturbed her, this time a sharp rapping. She sat upright, realizing first that she wasn't in either her mother's spare room, or her new bedroom in Kimberly Cottage. The events of the previous day came flooding back.

"Dymphna's house," she thought groggily. "Maybe it's just the old house settling." Another sharp tap-tap reached her. Then she heard quiet voices and it clicked - someone had knocked on the front door and been admitted. More than one, if she hadn't imagined that first, different rap. Now she strained her ears, she was sure she could hear people moving around downstairs. Good manners went to war with her curiosity. She was a guest in the Moriarty house and it was Dymphna's own business who came into her house and when, but it was the middle of the night...who on earth visited at this hour? She hesitated for a moment, but pure nosiness won in the end. She hopped out of the bed; felt for the slippers she had brought from home and cautiously opened her bedroom door.

The small landing was dark and the only light came from a lamp on the table in the hallway below. The old stairs wound around and down exactly like the one in her house, and Eve suspected it creaked just as much. She waited, listening intently, until she heard the faint sound of voices murmuring in the kitchen. Trying to match the squeaky steps to the rise and fall of the sound from below she made her way to the small lobby, the match of her own next door. As she paused for a moment to collect herself, she realized she had no real plan. She could hardly put her ear to the door and eavesdrop, could she? Maybe she should just go into Dymphna's sitting room and look at the books there, maybe borrow one to help her settle? And just as she decided to do just that, the door to the kitchen swung open, light pouring out into the hallway and Dymphna Moriarty said drily, "Would you not come in, Eve. It must be chilly in the hall."

# Chapter 7

Blushing furiously, Eve entered the kitchen with as much dignity as one can in a pair of borrowed pyjamas in the middle of the night. There were four women seated around an ancient but sturdy kitchen table, its surface well scrubbed over many years. Dymphna sat at the head of the table calmly pouring tea into an eclectic mix of mugs. Beside her sat a woman that Eve recognized as Claudia Warren, Jennie Warren's mother. On the other side was a short, round woman, with a wrinkled, smiley face and beside her, a slim small woman that Eve recognized immediately.

"Hi, Mam," Eve said politely.

"Hiya, love. Sit down there beside Claudia and have a cup of tea."

Eve obeyed, but said pointedly, "I didn't expect to see you here."

"Then you lack common sense, dear. Did you think I would sit at home twiddling my thumbs while my daughter was embroiled in a murder? Here, have a chocolate biscuit."

"Don't be annoyed with your poor mother," Claudia patted Eve on the arm gently. "If it was your daughter you wouldn't sit at home, not if you could help. We're all here to lend a hand."

Eve shook her head, touched but exasperated.

"There's nothing to be done, ladies. It's unfortunate that he chose my living room to meet his end, but I'm only a bystander. It's that teacher, Margaret, who should be worried. She's more than likely their prime suspect. And even if I was in trouble, there's nothing to be gained by sitting around in the middle of the night worrying about it. The Gardaí and the lawyers will sort it out, let them do their job."

A blank silence met this firm statement, followed by a gust of laughter. Eve sighed. She knew from experience her mother had never met a problem she didn't feel sure she could solve better herself and she could see the other ladies shared a similar level of self-belief.

"Ah, go on with yourself," the elderly apple cheeked woman grinned at Eve. "We're of more use to you than a barrel of lawyers and certainly a safer bet than waiting for the cops to figure it out. I'm a great admirer of our Gardaí, fine body of men and women and fierce good looking in their uniforms. But they don't know you and your family, and if things look bad against you - well, you don't want to be risking that, do you?"

"Greta's right," Dymphna said. "This is Greta Goode, Eve. But most people call her Granny."

"That's right. Granny Goode, that's me. I've been Granny since I was in my sixties, would you believe? A long time ago now, not that I look my age!" and she patted her hair complacently while Eve choked back a laugh.

"But what do you think you can do, ladies? I've a solicitor ready for tomorrow, thanks to Dymphna. I'm sure Claudia here can vouch for how competent she is. There's nothing else we can do."

"Oh yes there is," her mother said. "We can find out who

bumped off Brian O'Reilly."

There was a murmur of agreement from the other women. "We can find out why he was in your living room. And who hated him." Granny Goode chipped in.

"Dymphna is convinced this Margaret one is innocent," Claudia shook her head, "but I'm not so sure. If she lied about why she was on the scene, she could be lying about anything."

"You think she was lying about that too?" Eve couldn't help herself. "I was sure she was lying, you couldn't possibly see that the door was off the latch from the roadside and if you stepped inside someone's house to check on them, why would you almost close the door behind you? People don't, they leave it open so they don't look like they're snooping."

"Maybe it swung shut by itself..." Niamh offered, but Eve shook her head. "No, Mam, I checked it myself. If you half open it, it stays half open. It doesn't swing open or shut on its own." "Margaret couldn't hurt a fly," Dymphna insisted.

"I think there's more to Margaret than you think. I know I only met her today, but some of her story was true and some was fudged if not a downright lie." Eve added reluctantly, "I could *hear* it. Like, some rang true and other bits were echoey and unreal."

The other women exchanged a glance. Niamh looked smug. "I told you; Eve is very sensitive. She always was."

Eve blushed again. "I'm not. Not like you mean. I just don't think she's telling the full story." "Well then, we need to get the truth. Leave that to me," Dymphna said, "I'll get it out of her."

"Excellent." Niamh said. "We need to find out who had a motive to kill him. I know he was unpopular but outside of television programmes, no one bumps off the neighbours for petty reasons. Either he gave someone the serious hump, or he was in the wrong place and disturbed someone." "Which brings us to, why Kimberly? What were they doing there?"

"Has anyone considered Frances O'Reilly? She will inherit quite a tidy sum, from what I've heard. Brian was a miserly git, he wouldn't spend Christmas if he could help it. Yes, she stands to gain a lot."

"That young Garda, she told me Frances has an alibi. She was in work."

"I'll tackle her," Claudia said. "I know her through the Irish Women's Brigade. She's a junior member, not what I'd call Brigade material. Doesn't like getting her hands dirty and not what you'd call a charitable soul. But I can call around and offer condolences."

"Eve and I will find out everything we can about his connection to Kimberly Cottage. As the new owner, she can ask questions about the property without sounding suspicious. And we can ask your Orla, Dymphna." Niamh looked an inquiry at her old friend. "Yes, of course. I'll tell her to expect you. You should go see Maud Williams as well, she might know something. I know the O'Reillys were always hovering around. She detested them but was too polite for her own good."

"But we can't just go blundering around, interrogating people," Eve protested.

"Of course not," Granny Goode said scornfully. "We'll be *discreet*. I'll find out what the five-oh are thinking, get the intel. We need to get out in front of any charges Eve might be facing."

"She means she'll find out what the Gardaí are thinking," Dymphna translated to the group. "Yeah. Can't have the filth banging up one of our own." Granny smiled happily and munched on another biscuit.

"Um...thanks," Eve said weakly. Dymphna grinned and explained, "Granny's granddaughter is in the force. You met her today, Garda Maguire."

Eve dropped her head into her hands and groaned. "Okay. Of course. Of course, she's related to one of you. Tell me, Mrs. - I mean, *Granny* Goode. Is Garda Maguire aware you refer to the Gardaí Siochána as "the filth," a term I've only ever heard in dramas set in England among London criminals?"

"Who do you think taught me? She keeps me up to date on all the lingo. Have to keep relevant. My YouTube subscribers appreciate it." "Greta has the second most popular true crime video blog in Ireland," Niamh said proudly, "She'll have an army of loyal followers working on the case by lunch time tomorrow. And Garda Maguire too, of course."

Greta Goode graciously acknowledged the tribute with a nod. "Between us we've a lot to bring to the table. And that's just the mundane skills. If we have to, we'll boil up a couple of frogs and start terrorizing the neighbourhood." "Well, let's hope it won't come to that," Dymphna said.

Eve could only agree. The old women were terrifying enough without adding in their occult skills. Claudia was adept at a range of potions and was an expert at coaxing information from people. Eve suspected Dymphna was equally at home with herbs, but also seemed to be able to influence people, with her uncanny, mesmerizing eyes. Her mother, she knew, had a reputation as a healer but the flip side of that was always the ability to do the opposite. Heal or Hex, as the old saying went. She wasn't sure where Granny Goode's skill set lay but she was absolutely sure she would prefer not to know. The old woman looked up suddenly, caught her eye then chuckled and winked, confirming Eve's determination to avoid letting the lot of them loose on the neighbourhood.

"I appreciate the help, I do. If you insist on poking around, that's one thing but whatever we find should go straight to Detective Desmond. Agreed?"

The four older women all nodded assent readily enough, which strangely did nothing to reassure her. "Well, I'm off home." Eve's mother came over and embraced her. "I'll be around in the morning. Your brother will drive me. Go back to bed now and get sleep. You'll need it." All the visitors agreed it was time to leave. Eve hovered until Dymphna had shown them out, then faced her host. "I'm really sorry. I had no business coming downstairs and intruding, it was very rude of me." Dymphna laughed. "I would have done the same myself. It's in our nature. Pure nosey, that's a sure sign."

"I'm not...I'm not like ye," Eve began, but her neighbour just grinned. By the time she'd climbed upstairs, and made her way back to bed, Eve was conscious of being exhausted again. Snuggling in she hardly registered the time, just the warmth of the bed and the quiet peace of the cottage. The next thing she knew sunshine was streaming through the window and her phone was ringing. She sat bolt upright trying to get the screen to open to answer it. Finally she managed to swipe the right way, cursing under her breath. What a way to wake up! Annoyance flooded her as she wondered who could be so rude as to ring her so early in the morning. It was - oh, wow, it was half past nine in the morning. She tried to focus on the voice at the other end of the line, a rather exasperated sounding man asking, "Can you hear me, Ms. Caulton?"

"Um. Sorry, yes. I was asleep, sorry." "Oh. Well, this is Detective Cullen. We'd like you to come into the station to give a statement. As soon as possible, please. As you can imagine, time is of the essence in these cases."

"Ah. Yes. Well, I'll come as soon as my solicitor is free, thanks."

His voice became a touch frosty. "Do you feel you need a solicitor to accompany you?"

"Yes, I do." Eve replied firmly. "My lawyer told me yesterday to only attend with her and I have no intention of ignoring her advice. I'll let you know when to expect us."

There was a pause. The back of Eve's neck tingled and she would have bet good money the detective was consulting someone else on his end of the call.

"Fair enough. Ring me back."

Eve flopped back down on the bed and groaned.

"I don't think I'm making a good impression," she thought. Feeling horribly nervous, she rang Jennie Warren. "Have they called you in?" Warren didn't waste time with preliminaries.

"Yes, as soon as we can. I said I would come when you were free."

"Good girl. Well, get yourself ready and I'll pick you up in an hour. Brace yourself, Eve. The fun starts now."

# Chapter 8

Eve was at her neighbour's kitchen table and sipping coffee before she realized what awaited her outside. She had vaguely noted that Dymphna's front curtains remained firmly closed, despite the bright morning. It was only when she had woken up a bit more that she heard the noise. The shouting was like a continuous grumble, an unending round of "Eve! Eve!" mixed with "Did you know the dead man?" "Come on, Mrs. Moriarty!" and "Cash for Interviews!" She looked at Dymphna who simply said, "Reporters." It was the same tone of voice she would have used to say "vermin."

The idea of leaving the house and facing a gauntlet of cameras and microphones turned her stomach. Her hostess shrugged and took the view that there was no way around it. "If you hide, they'll go after you like terriers. If you talk to them, they'll twist everything. Best just carry on as if they're not there. In fact, imagine them not being there. They'll soon disappear."

Eve had tried to be sanguine and to her relief her solicitor offered to pick her up but the run from the door to Jennie Warren's car had been horrible. It was short spin to the Merrion Garda Station but the drive gave her time to compose herself.

The interview room was every bit as intimidating as Eve had expected. It was dingy, but clean; there was a table with a pair of chairs on either side. She had seen versions of this on so many crime shows, it almost looked familiar. But what television couldn't show was the grim atmosphere, the airless stuffiness of the room, and the tension. She had walked in with Jennie Warren, who turned out to be a pretty redhead with a wry sense of humour and a confident air. A polite desk sergeant had shown them to the room and asked if they wanted anything to drink. They had both requested coffees, he had withdrawn and neither coffee nor cops had come near them since. That had been over forty minutes ago.

"Don't worry," Jennie was busying herself with files, taking the chance to catch up on paperwork. "It's a tactic. Try to relax."

How? Eve thought. It was nerve wracking She was aware of her bum going numb, but wondered if she started pacing the room, would it look like she was nervous and guilty? If she needed to use the bathroom, would they let her? And of course, the moment that thought crossed her mind, she began to feel like she could do with going to the loo. The joy of being fifty after two kids, she thought. She wondered if the lovely Liza, Peter's new wife, the new Mrs. Dunne, ever needed to use the toilet facilities at short notice. She bet not. Liza was in her thirties or at least claimed to be. She was definitely slim and as fit as a fiddle. A sudden thought hit her. Did Peter know about the murder? Mairead and Liam would have told him, surely. It would have been on the news, too. Did he worry at all about her? She knew the answer, if she was honest. He was probably terrified his golfing buddies would find out. She shifted uncomfortably in the seat, hoping the change in position would stop her back from giving out.

Finally the door opened to admit both Ronan Desmond and

Detective Cullen. The older man carried a tray, with two coffees. Desmond greeted Eve by name, then turned to her solicitor. "Ms. Warren," he said coldly. "How interesting." "Calm yourself, Detective." She grinned at him, and added, "Don't be reading too much into my presence here. Ms. Caulton is a friend of my mother's. I'm here as a courtesy."

"I see. I thought she wasn't your usual type of client." Detective Cullen said.

"She's my favourite type of client, Detective. Innocent."

"I thought all your clients were "*innocent*"" he said with a full measure of snark.

Jennie smiled sweetly. "They're usually found innocent in a court of law, aren't they?"

Eve snorted with laughter but hastily changed it to a cough. She glanced at Ronan Desmond. His face was composed but his eyes were twinkling. Even Cullen didn't seem genuinely annoyed at Jennie. She was sure he liked the woman, under his blustering tone.

"Shall we get started, gentlemen? My client and I have waited some time. Without refreshments."

"Sorry," Ronan said sheepishly. "There was a bit of an incident, out in the public waiting room. It was all hands on deck. The sergeant had his hands full." "Let's crack on, anyway." Cullen sat back in his chair and stared at Eve. "Ms. Caulton, I understand you moved into Kimberly Cottage on... Tuesday morning?" "Yes."

"So, three days ago. And on the second day, a neighbour of yours is found dead in your house. Murdered."

"Yes."

"Any idea why? Why your house, and why he died?" "No, none."

The detectives exchanged a look.

"And you are sure you never met Brian O'Reilly before he called to the door of Kimberly Cottage on Tuesday afternoon?"

"I am absolutely positive."

"Ms. Caulton, are you sure you didn't leave your front door unlocked?" "Positive," Eve said firmly. "Once I had time to think about it, I recalled hearing the door click into place."

"Hmm. How convenient, to remember so clearly after the fact. Can you explain why your back door was unlocked?"

Eve was startled. "Was it? Yesterday? Oh. No, I'm sorry. I don't recall opening it at all yesterday. But it's possible, or I may simply have forgotten to lock it the previous night."

"You may have left it unlocked." Detective Desmond made it sound like an accusation.

"Anyone have spare keys to that door?"

"There's only one key to the back door." Eve had intended to have a few spares cut but there simply hadn't been time, she had moved in so quickly. "You can ask the estate agents, Orla Moriarty is the one I deal with. She knows I only received one back door key, and a double set of front door keys." She looked at Jennie anxiously.

"My client has already answered, Detective. Front door shut when she left, open when she returned. Back door, she has no idea. It's her house, after all. It's not a crime to leave your back door accidentally unlocked."

"I _do_ think I locked it Tuesday night," Eve offered. "But I could have overlooked it."

"I see. Let's start again. Wednesday afternoon. You were unpacking and then what? Just decided to go for a walk?"

And around and around they went. The questions varied in style, format and delivery but at the heart they remained

57

the same. What was Brian doing in her house, and why was he killed? It was wearying and as the day wore on, she was increasingly glad that she had brought Jennie Warren with her. It was easy to get confused and tired, and the slightest deviation in wording or tone set one or other of the detectives off, nit-picking every word until she was half unsure herself what she meant to say.

"Enough," Jennie declared after yet another re-telling of the same basic facts. "My client has had a terrible shock, witnessed a scene of violent death and has barely slept. She's in shock. This is a voluntary statement and despite your best efforts, she's told you consistently - she doesn't know anything. Now, unless you've anything else to ask her - something *new*, Detectives - I think we need to bring this to a close."

Eve resisted the urge to fall weeping on the lawyer's shoulder but only just. The detectives excused themselves briefly, obviously to consult in private, and returned to say once the statement was signed, Eve was free to go. Jennie insisted on reading it through, twice, before she was satisfied but at last, they were allowed to leave, emerging into late afternoon sunshine.

"Oh, my heavens." Eve managed, as soon as they were safely out of earshot.

"Bet you're glad you weren't alone," Jennie smiled. "I would have been absolutely lost, Jennie. I can't thank you enough. It was scary and relentless and I got so confused, I'm sure they think I'm guilty."

The solicitor shook her shiny red bob. "No, quite the opposite. Criminals and guilty people rehearse their statements so much, they don't vary by a syllable. Cullen and Desmond are experienced, capable investigators. They were satisfied by the end. You did extremely well."

Relief hit Eve like a hammer and for the first time since finding Margaret standing over Brian's body, she allowed herself to just wallow for a few minutes. Blinking back tears, she drew a shaky breath. Jennie patted her arm. "It's okay. You've been through a lot in the last 24 hours. Let's get you home."

# Chapter 9

Garda Maguire was waiting outside Kimberly Cottage as they pulled up. A few stragglers remained from the morning's news frenzy but a glare from the Garda kept them quiet and at a distance. Next door in Vespertilio Cottage, Dymphna hovered near the door. Eve thanked Jennie profusely and pressed her to send an invoice as soon as convenient.

"You're worth every penny," Eve told her. "Well, it's my pleasure. Mam wouldn't want me to charge you, though. You know what that lot are like. "Be of use," and "Do your bit," not to mention, "I was forty hours in labour with you, you owe me!" Eve laughed. "Yeah well, I prefer to pay cash. Never mind your mother." "Easy for you to say. Look, we'll work something out. In the meantime, mind yourself and ring me if you need me." Garda Maguire greeted her with a smile. "Ms. Caulton. Forensics is finished with your house; you can go back in."

Eve eyed the cottage. "I'm not sure I want to," she blurted out. Garda Maguire nodded sympathetically. "Ah, I can understand that. But sure, I'll come in with you. We'll soon have the place back in order, and I'm sure Mrs. Moriarty would like to help too." Dymphna appeared at Eve's elbow. "I will of course," She nudged Eve. "Let's see this crime scene, then." "That crime scene happens to be my living room," Eve pointed out.

"And it's still your living room, dear. It's just also a crime scene now. Have to be practical about these things." Dymphna prodded her over the doorstep and into the living room."

The pile of books was more or less as she had left them, although the ones over which Brian O'Reilly's corpse had sprawled had obviously been interfered with. The Gardaí had been reasonably careful though. Eve had half expected an epic mess, but this was no worse than the unpacking she had left. "It's not as bad as I feared," She remarked.

"Ah, we try not to leave the place in heap," Garda Maguire pointed at the piles of books by the side of the sofa. "The crime scene lot went through everything, but they're book-lovers to a man, or woman. You won't find any cracked spines or torn pages. And I heard Detective Desmond insist that they be careful too. It's rotten luck on you, moving in and having this happen."

Eve was touched. After the grueling day it was nice to be treated with a little thoughtfulness. It seemed Jennie Warren had been right, the Gardaí were only doing their job and it wasn't personal.

"Where do you want us to start?" Garda Maguire asked.

"With a cup of tea. Or coffee, as preferred. "Eve replied firmly. "Sod all this, let's at least have a biscuit in us before we tackle it."

Hot tea and a few decent biscuits did a lot to restore her spirits and break the ice. After tea they turned to tidying, Garda Maguire lending a helping hand. By the time the books were neatly on the shelves, Eve had heard all about Joanne Maguire's family, friends, and career prospects. Some time was devoted to the complicated power dynamics between her and her handsome but stuffy colleague, Garda Aloysius Hickey.

Hickey was from Co. Clare and felt himself a cut above mere Dubliners. He had played GAA Football for his county, and was a fluent Irish speaker. Jo Maguire was a Dubliner, hated team sports and had only schoolgirl Irish. On her side, however, she was great at dealing with people, popular in the Merrion Station, and had a phenomenal memory. She recounted several juicy anecdotes about cases, ending with her favourite moment of triumph over her colleague.

"Hickey walked right past him, but the minute I clocked his weaselly little face, I remembered it. Fancy McGuigan, Dublin's most inept shoplifter. Brother of the accused and wanted on ten counts of being caught on CCTV helping himself to items in local shops. Well, once we had him booked, the brother panicked and rolled over. It was brilliant! Hickey almost choked when he heard."

She laughed merrily, happy to have an appreciative audience for once. Eve laughed out loud and congratulated her on a victory over her country colleague. The time passed pleasantly enough and soon a neat bookcase emerged from the mess.

Eve stepped back and surveyed the end result. "Well, that's a lot better! I can't thank you both enough."

"Our pleasure," Garda Maguire pointed towards the right hand side of one of the many bookshelves lining the walls. This one was beside the large bow window, and where the shelves met the edge of the window, there was an ornate panel. But at the very top, one of the panels hung slightly askew, its carved Celtic knot hanging tipsily. "You've one panel out of place there, Eve. It must have happened as we were pushing books up on that shelf. Hang on there and I'll hop up, put it back in place."

She matched word to action, and was up the rather rickety step-ladder Eve had pressed into service to reach the highest shelve. "I've got it, just need to give it a shove..." then she said in quite a different tone of voice, "Oh! Eve, it's not loose. It's on hinges, it's meant to move. There's probably a spring, and we managed to push on it by accident. I can just see inside... there's something in here!" "What is it?" Both Dymphna and Eve replied in chorus. "Hang on..." Jo fished about until she produced a small package, about six inches by four inches, wrapped in what looked like oilskin. "It feels like a book!"

Eve cleared the coffee table, and Jo laid her treasure on it carefully.

"You open it, Eve, it's your house."

Eve unwrapped it with reverence, revealing a small leather-bound book, with a beautiful pattern worked into the cover, letters picked out in gilt and tiny embellishments in jewel tones twinkling in the light." "Oh, it's so pretty," She exclaimed, the artist in her delighted by the decoration and attractive colours. She angled it to get a better look. "It says, "*Julia O'Reilly 1911,*" and underneath, "*From Constantine.*" The three women stared at the small journal.

"1911," breathed Jo. "That's older even than you, Mrs. Moriarty."

"Cheeky brat. I wonder who she was? Maud Williams is 90, or thereabouts. She bought this house when she got married, back in the nineteen sixties. I know, because she told me all about it. I moved here with my husband in nineteen seventy two, and Maud was a newcomer like me. We bonded very quickly, because all the other neighbours were older. But if she ever told me who lived here before them, or who they bought the place from, I've long forgotten."

Eve opened the diary, very gently and paying great care not to pull at the spine or dislodge anything. There was a frontispiece, in ornate Celtic knot-work, with the year and a place to write your name. This was filled in with "Julia O'Reilly," followed by page upon page of flowing, cursive handwriting. "My Dad had writing like that," Dymphna said, "Imagine learning that in school nowadays. My Grand-kids can barely write, they're so used to laptops and phones."

"I think the whole thing is handmade," Eve said, thoroughly impressed. "I think someone made this for "Julia," including the cover, as a gift. Look at the tiny stitching, holding the pages in. And that frontispiece was printed by hand, I'm sure of it."

"It's a little work of art. And of history." Jo remarked. "I bet a local library or history group would love it!"

"Maybe we'll pass it on," Eve agreed, "But first I want to read it! I'm dying to know who she was and why it was hidden up there."

"How long do you think it was tucked up there?"

"I don't know, but the wrappings are nearly perished. Maybe it'll be clearer once I've read it."

"There you go now," Jo nudged her with a grin, "We were meant to find it. It'll take your mind off things, deciphering that handwriting. I'll have to get off now, but let me know what you find out from it. Bye, Mrs. Moriarty. Bye, Eve." The Garda paused at the door and added, "Did you notice her surname? Julia O'Reilly. Think it's a coincidence?"

Eve blinked. "Oh. You mean, Brian O'Reilly...surely it can't be connected? What could some diary from 1911 have to do with a murder in 2022?"

"Well, O'Reilly was looking for something in your living room," Jo pointed out. "Maybe this was it."

She left the two other women nonplussed, staring at the pages of writing and wondering, could this possibly be the key to whatever was going on in Bramble Lane?

# Chapter 10

I t was much later that evening before Eve had time to do more than glance at the mysterious journal. While putting the sitting room back to order and finishing the book unpacking had helped, it definitely would have felt a bit odd to sit reading in the room in which someone had so recently died. Without thinking too much about it she retreated to her bedroom with a cup of tea and decided to curl up in bed, her own bed tonight, and read the first entries. They might at least clear up the identity of the writer and the "Constantine" on the front cover.

Mrs. Moriarty had agreed when she said she wanted to return home, but made Eve promise to return if she felt in any way scared or uncomfortable.

"Don't wait for an invitation, Eve. And don't sit in there feeling scared."

"Better to jump back in," Eve replied, "but yes, if I get spooked I'll be around."

She opened the diary and started to read, taking her time over the old-fashioned calligraphy. The first page reiterated the information on the front cover, with some additions:

"*To my Dearest Julia, from your Constantine,*" with a date - December 21st, 1911. The Midwinter Solstice, Eve thought. And "your Constantine" probably meant they were a courting couple. How romantic!

The first entry was short.

*"I am so grateful to Con for this gift. It was kindly intentioned, and even more kindly executed. I know the hours of careful toil that have been spent, creating this. His poor eyes, already strained by his studies, shut up in that dim room, pouring over medical text books! Then instead of his well-earned rest, he has laboured over leather, and paper, with needle and thread, just to make this for me. My heart is full."*

On the next page, there was a dated entry:

*"December 23rd. I had meant to write daily, as Con suggested, but I have made a poor start, I fear. It was not my fault, however. Yesterday Mother was in such a melancholy mood, nothing would cheer her but to have the entire cottage cleaned from attic to floor. She misses the excitement of Christmas in the old house, where she had an army of staff to order around and a hundred tasks to oversee, as Mistress. I cannot wonder at her dismay, to be reduced to a workman's cottage, although for my part I have no regrets. Father is sorely missed of course, but he would have approved of all Uncle has done, I am sure. If I had known last Christmas that I would be so grateful to Uncle William! I am ashamed of how I disliked him, and thought him mean. His manner is gruff and disapproving but nothing could have been kinder than his actions, when poor Father died. We could be penniless, and homeless and instead we are safe here in this sweet cottage. Kimberly Cottage, I wonder who named it? We are grateful for our neighbours, and I am most particularly so –if we had not moved here, if our neighbours had not been so kind, I would not have met Constantine, Dear Con. I told Mother, all will be well. I cannot tell her why I am so certain, of course, but soon I will be able to reveal my secret. Til then, I will do all I can to*

67

*make her happy."*

Eve smiled. So, Constantine was indeed a suitor. And Julia O'Reilly had been a "young lady" in a big house, until her father died. Quite a story, like one of her mother's favourite period romances. She continued to read. The subsequent entries were very domestic, records of visitors who called to wish them well at Christmas, descriptions of Julia's neighbours, her mother (who was frequently "melancholy" or as Eve thought, querulous and demanding") and some allusions to "her secret." It was an entry dated in February of 1912 that gave some more concrete information.

*"A bad day today. Sad, and hard. It started well enough, I was able to do the laundry with the help of Kathleen. Her mother has been so kind, patient with the silly girl who cannot do any of the household tasks the women of Bramble lane take for granted. Lending me Kathleen to help means more work for Nellie but under her care, I have learned to cook tolerably well, to blacken a stove, tend the hearth and now, wash, starch, dry, and press sheets and bedding. However, through no fault of Kathleen's, I somehow managed to damage Mother's precious Spanish shawl. I was so careful, and it truly needed a wash, but either the water was too hot, or I did something wrong in the drying. At any rate it has dried "out of shape"and Mama was most upset. Furious, in fact, at my carelessness and stupidity. She has so few nice things left, and it is so hard for her. As she says, she cannot bear to see her only daughter skivvying. I confess, I was hard in return, and so far forgot myself as to be sharp and unkind with her."*

*"Then she brought up Constantine, and her words wounded me so deeply, I came too close to blurting out the truth. She sees only the son of a workman, with an accent that marks his class and clothes that show his straightened means. I cannot persuade her to look*

*beneath and see his kindness, his determination to succeed. He has been accepted into the school of medicine, on his own merit, because of his brains and character! He helps his father too, whenever he can, and has showered us with so many kindnesses – Mother overlooks all the times he has fixed things in the house, and outside, without recompense. We cannot afford to pay a handyman to do these things."*

"Mother" was a selfish auld cow, Eve thought, and a snob. But she supposed back in those far off days things like class and accent mattered. She was sleepy now, but read one last entry before slipping into a deep, dreamless sleep.

*"Yesterday I felt so sad and hopeless, but how foolish of me! Today I saw Con leaving for his rounds at the Hospital, I slipped out and managed some few words with him at the garden gate. How sensible he is, how patient. "Whenever you are ready," he said. What sweet words. He understands how I feel when I can hardly explain myself, to myself. He looked tired, but denies that he is overdoing things. I will make it my daily duty to watch his health. Hospitals are treacherous places, and I will not let him fall ill while trying to help others." "In a few months he will be Dr. Constantine Farrell. How glad we shall be when that day comes."*

True love, Eve thought as she slipped asleep.

Claudia Warren, Granny Goode and Garda Jo Maguire joined Eve, Dymphna and Niamh in an impromptu meeting the next morning, squeezing into Eve's sitting room and listening eagerly to the story of the diary and its contents. Eve had tried to put them off, but the older ladies had simply ignored her. There was no way they were missing out on this exciting, new development, even if it had nothing to do with the murder. Jo advised her, "Give in, it's easier in the long run. I know, from experience."

69

"Bunch of old bats," Eve grumbled but she was quite glad of the company. Somehow the energy and spirit of the women made the place feel more and more ...safe. Safe and homely. She resigned herself to the inevitable and opened a packet of good biscuits.

"So, there's more entries after that but they're all daily events. Interesting, but nothing more about Constantine and Julia. Until we hit May 1912. Here we are....it's a long entry, starting with the morning,"

"*It is finally here. I can hardly bring myself to believe it. The day Constantine officially becomes Dr. Farrell. He will no longer have to pose as a single man, and I can finally break the news to dear Mama. It will be a shock to her, I know. It is a pity she has not adjusted better to our new life. If she was more accepting of our changed circumstances, she would be happier. Even Uncle William has repeatedly advised her to be more adaptable – as he says, all he can provide for us has been given and there is no more to be done. But surely, when presented with a son in law who is DOCTOR rather than (in her eyes) a "mere" labourer – surely that must be some comfort to her. Con has his own family to care for, but says one more makes no difference. He and I will work to build up his practice and Mother will be taken care of. Oh, how I have longed for our life together to begin.*"

The entry continued but there had obviously been a gap of several hours between the optimism of the morning and this scribbled continuation.

"*Ah. I can hardly bear to write. When I have done, I will do as Con advised and hide this journal. I will no longer entrust myself, or my plans, to my mother's power. For all her faults, and I am not blind to them, I had thought her possessed of a loving heart. That she could be so heartless, so cruel, I would not allow myself*" *to believe." "Constantine arrived home this afternoon to much fanfare and cheer, the whole community turning out to celebrate his achievement. I attended but hung back, being in such a position as made it impossible to be natural. My heart was pounding, fit to break my chest. He lost no time in taking his parents aside and breaking the news to them. His mother burst into tears, then laughed, then hugged him. His father had some serious words to say – after all, he cannot approve our deceit no matter how well-intentioned. He was also worried about Con burdening himself with a wife at such an early stage of his career. But in the end, all was smiles and congratulations, and much that was kind."*

*"But we still had my mother to face, and we chose to do so immediately. Mr. and Mrs. Farrell offered to help, to soften the blow with their presence but I declined. In the first violence of her reaction, Mother was likely to say things she would regret, and might offend and wound them. It was better that we suffer the initial storm and let her have time to come to our way of thinking. I am so glad we did, for it was worse – far worse – than I imagined."*

The women heaved a collective sigh. "I knew that auld wagon would cut up rough," Granny Goode interjected, "She must have been a right auld Tartar."

"Hush. Anyway, it continues..."

*"No sooner had we revealed our secret, that I was not her unmarried daughter, nor had I been since the previous year, that I was in fact the proud wife of the new Dr. Farrell, than she went into hysterics. It took a good half hour, and many efforts on our part, to restore her to quietness. Even then, her invective was unabated. She called Con names that made me glad his parents were absent, and called me names I will not repeat nor suffer myself to remember. Indeed, I am half convinced she was deranged in the moment, to use such language. Con reassured her that we had no*

*intention of abandoning her, that we would be a support to her if only she would let us, that his prospects were unusually bright having gained the friendship and patronage of one of his lecturers and good recommendations from all. Instead of being grateful or relieved, she became instantly enraged. What? the great Mrs. O'Reilly, daughter in law of Judge O'Reilly, niece to Mr. Boyd of Roscommon House, be a pensioner on the charity of (I will not repeat the terms here applied to my poor Con.) – no, it would not be borne."*

*"And then, the crux of it came – while Con and I are married, we have not yet started our married life in earnest. Once she realized that, she became smug. "You are not in fact married then!" she snapped, "and you never will be. I shall contact your Uncle immediately and he will have this nonsense annulled." I grew frightened then, although Con laughed at her. Such was her anger, we were forced to part again for tonight, and he will return tomorrow. She agreed to see him, on condition that I stay here with her for the moment."*

Eve looked around her rapt audience. "Poor Julia," she said with feeling, "That woman is a monster!"

"It was the times, though," Claudia pointed out. "Life was hard, social classes were rigid. It's easy to judge but it was normal for young women in every sphere of life to be ordered about by their parents. People rarely married without consent, and certainly it was normal to wait until you had some money set aside, not set out in life so young." "I thought everyone married in their teens back then," Jo said.

"No, quite the opposite. People couldn't afford to marry young and those that did soon fell into poverty. No birth control, high infant mortality, living hand to mouth…and if Uncle William objected to the marriage or was offended by the elopement he could throw the Mother out of the cottage. She was probably afraid." "Hmm. Well, I still think she was a mean, selfish woman," Eve replied. She turned to the next page and resumed the story.

"*It has been almost a week since I hid this record, in a cubbyhole Con devised months ago. He did so for fun, but it has proved most useful. On the night we told my mother of our news, she sent for Uncle William. He arrived late and was closeted with her for an hour. What she said to him, I can only imagine. He left without speaking to me, but in the morning, Mother informed me that he will start legal proceedings to annul my marriage. I am to be sent to my cousins in England, to "make myself useful," and will not be allowed return until I have come to my senses. I pointed out that she will find it hard to manage without me - I have no doubt I am being sent to skivvy for my cousins, but I have been in the same role here for a year now. Who would do the housework? She smiled, such a smile, and said that Uncle is anxious to avoid scandal and attention and has agreed to provide her with a maid while I am away.*" "*There is now a frightening prospect ahead of me. My cousins live in a remote, isolated area. If I am bundled up and sent there, like unwanted baggage, it will be hard to return not least because they are miserly and closefisted. I will receive no wage nor allowance. My mother will be satisfied with a maid in my place. A maid instead of her loving, devoted daughter!*

*Only Con and his family will care for my well-being, and they will not be able to trace me. I am trapped behind locked doors, my mother my gaoler. Uncle has made it clear that if I rebel further, he will hand me over to the Nuns as a wanton, a spoiled and disgraced woman.*

*All I can do is try to get word to Con. If I fail, I may never see him again. If I succeed, I will never step foot in this house again. Not while Mother lives, at any rate. I miss my father today, he was stern but kind. I pray he will reach out his hand to me, and aid me now. Oh, Con! Please be wide awake, and ready for action.*"

Eve looked up. "That's it, that's the last entry."

# Chapter 11

"Oh my god," Dymphna breathed. "Well, I saw it myself. Long after Julia O'Reilly there were plenty of young girls put away for being troublesome. It was a very real possibility, right up to the nineteen seventies. She must have been terrified."

"Kimberly Cottage certainly has a lot of secrets," Eve replied. "Is it possible that this is what Brian was looking for? Is it coincidence they were O'Reilly's?" "He was always wild to buy this place," Dymphna mused. "I can't see why anyone would kill over the diary, but on the other hand I don't believe in this much coincidence. You were meant to find that book, Eve. I think Julia is trying to tell you something."

"Eh, stop right there. It's bad enough my house is a crime scene without you adding in friendly ghosts. Let's keep an open mind. And we should visit Maud Williams as soon as possible, see if she can remember anything that might help."

"Come on, you lot. We all know what we have to work on - let's get to it."

The women went their separate ways. Eve was relieved to see the media had largely deserted the Lane; other stories were moving faster and needed their attention. They would be back at some point, she was sure, but for now Bramble Lane was peaceful.

Armed with the address and a note from Dymphna introducing them, Eve and her mother presented themselves at Willowbrook Nursing home just as afternoon visiting commenced. It soon became evident that the home had very strict regulations about visitors, and at first the reception nurse was inclined to dismiss them. Niamh smiled at her, and started to talk, quietly and in a gentle rhythmic tone. Eve could sense the nurse relax and wasn't surprised when she agreed suddenly that Maud would *love* a visit, and they should use the small library room, where they would be undisturbed. Many a teacher had entered a parent-teacher meeting with Niamh Caulton armed with a set of complaints, only to exit wondering how they had ever misunderstood the lovely Caulton children.

They sat in the library room, waiting. The door opened to admit an orderly wheeling a chair in which sat a white-haired woman, with a sweet and youthful face. She was very frail, a tiny bird of a woman, but her eyes were alert and intelligent. She read Dymphna's note quickly and looked expectantly at Eve.

"Are you here about the murder, pet? Sure, I don't know what I can tell you. But I'm happy to help if I can."

"It's sort of about the murder, but not entirely. I'm so sorry to intrude on you, but we're trying to piece things together and thought you might be able to answer some questions about Kimberly Cottage - its history, previous owners."

"Ah. You're trying to figure out why Brian O'Reilly was in your living room."

Eve was impressed. Maud clearly had her faculties, despite being ill.

"That's it exactly. I wondered if there was a connection

between him and the house, or some reason he might be anxious to gain access to it. I think, and it's just a theory, I think he was looking for something." "It's possible," Maud considered. "He was such an interfering, busybody of a man that it's possible he was just nosy. But looking back, he was always trying to gain entry. He only moved to Bramble Lane ten years ago, you know. Bought the Bolger's cottage when old Mr. Bolger died. Changed the name from Tivoli Cottage to "The O'Reilly Residence,"

All three women muttered, "Notions!"

"The moment he moved in he started throwing his weight around. He and that wife of his. Frances, that's her name. Constantly bothering me, if I'm honest. He started by saying I should give him a spare set of keys to mind, in case of emergency. I gave him short shrift on that one, I can tell you." Her eye's sparkled. "I let him know that Dymphna Moriarty had my spare set, thank you very much. He was quite put out. He said he was only trying to be neighbourly, which might be true but I doubt it."

Niamh Caulton asked, "Did he ever try to push in, or hang around when you were out?"

"I wasn't out much, maybe twice a week. He was always out in his garden, morning and evening, watching everyone come and go. It drove him wild that Ronan Desmond wouldn't tell him any private information, but he wheedled it out of everyone else. He was relentless. Just, a truly obnoxious and nosey man."

"What about Frances?"

"Highly neurotic. She works in some boutique, in the Merrion Shopping Centre. Posh kind of a place, the kind with only three styles of dresses in two colours with a large price tag. It's five minutes walk away so she was always trying to park her car in my driveway rather than leave it out on the road." "Yeah, he tried to persuade me to park my car out and let her use the drive," Eve grinned,

"I hope you told him to go boil his head! I was a fool to put up with his nonsense. But he wore me down, to be honest. I avoided him as much as possible, and when it dawned on me how much he wanted to get into the house, I'm afraid I became quite stubborn. Never invited him in, ever."

"Good for you," Niamh agreed. "And was it empty for long when you moved in here?" "No, I had a niece stay there for a few months. She and her friends wouldn't take any nonsense from Brian. After that it was empty for about two weeks, which is when you saw it and put in an offer. And may I say, I was delighted."

Eve smiled. "I love the place, despite the murder. But let's go back further. When you moved in, were you told anything about the previous owners?"

"Ah. Now, there I might be able to help you," Maud indicated a call button on the wall. "Give that a buzz will you, get that young man back here. I need to get something from my room."

It took a good fifteen minutes, but Maud returned clutching a blue folder. "It's all in here! I always did keep good records. My Declan used to remark on it all the time. "Maud will know," he'd say, if there was ever a question about something. "She never throws out receipts or correspondence."" Her eyes twinkled. "He couldn't fill out a form, bless him, used to get nervous at the sight of one. One of us had to be organized, am I right?"

Her hands shook a little as she undid the bobbin that held the folder shut. "Here, you look, Dear." She pushed the folder across to Eve. "I'm too slow, these days. In there, in a white

78

envelope, marked "house." That's it. Put them out on the coffee table." Eve spread the sheets of paper out so they could be see clearly.

"Now the larger sheets there, that's the deed of sale. But those letters, they're from when we bought the house. We found some bits and pieces in that attic, some small antique vases that looked valuable and a small table, quite ornate. It was for a bedroom, you'd put a pitcher of water and a washbowl on it. Before indoor plumbing. We wanted to ask if the previous owners wanted it."

Eve glanced at the letter. It was written on a small sheet of cream notepaper, embossed with a pretty floral border. It was brief, and to the point. "*Dear Mrs. Williams,*

*Thank you for your note. I appreciate your thoughtfulness, but the items you describe are of no interest to us. If they are of any use or value to you, please feel free to keep them or sell them as you choose. I hope you will be very happy in Kimberly Cottage, and please accept my congratulations on your recent nuptials.*

*Yours sincerely –* "

Eve looked up, excitement evident her face. "The signature!" She showed the note to her mother. "Yours sincerely.... Mrs. J Farrell"

Maud smiled at them. "Does that mean something to you?"

Eve and Niamh smiled back. "We have quite a little romance to tell you, Maud. It started with a diary we found..."

Some time later, the story faithfully recounted, they left Maud with promises to let her know if they found anything out about Julia and her husband. Maud was tired, her frailty obvious but her eyes were bright and the nurse whispered to them as they left, "She enjoyed your visit, I can tell."

"We must pop in again," Niamh remarked once they were on

the road back to Merrion and Bramble Lane. "She was a lovely old woman." Eve glanced at her mother in amusement. "She's only about ten years older than you, you know?"

"It's an important ten years, pet. Once you're over ninety, it's probably time to slow down a bit."

"It might be time to start practicing that in your mid eighties, Mam."

"Don't you try that on me, Eve. At my age, you do whatever you want and as often as you can or you'll seize up. Mentally as well as physically. I refuse to be older than I feel."

Eve patted her mother's arm. "We wouldn't change you, you know that. You're an inspiration. Plus you acting like you're fifty means I get to pretend I'm only in my thirties. Win-win situation."

"Hah! Well, I'm glad to see you out living a bit. Even if it took a murder to shake you up. I was beginning to be afraid you'd given up and were going to settle down to a life as a reclusive artist." "Ah, I'm not that bad." Eve replied.

"When was the last time you went out, even to meet friends?"

Eve opened her mouth to protest but shut it again. "I don't know, " She admitted. "It's not because I don't want to go out, it's just everyone is busy. It's not easy to find the time."

"And they're in couples," Niamh said bluntly. "They don't mean to exclude you, I know, but it can be a case of not wanting to make you feel awkward. You need new friends, pet."

Eve shrugged but in her heart she knew her mother was right. She needed people to hang around with, maybe even develop some new interests. Her arty friends were lovely but rarely available. When she was lecturing regularly, her work colleagues were very sociable but now she was semi-retired, she felt quite out of the loop. Yes, it was time to expand her friend group.

"What about you, Mam," she asked mischievously. "You seem to have a picked up your friendship with Dymphna quite nicely."

"I'm delighted," Niamh replied. "I see Claudia quite often, but catching up with Dymphna and Greta Goode has been so much fun. Now there are women who know how to live. Nothing puts a halt to their gallop, I can tell you. You could learn a lot from them."

"I'm beginning to see that."

"And don't roll your eyes at me when I say this, not like you usually do. You have a talent, Eve Caulton. You pretend to ignore it, you don't seem to trust it, but you should. It's a crying shame to see you waste it, and you have never even allowed Mairead or Liam understand our family traditions. That's your business which is why I've never interfered but you should respect the skills you learned and - and you should teach your kids to respect them. There, that's all I'm going to say about the matter." She sniffed then added, "Except to say, you can fight it all you want. In the end, you're as much a Boyd as a Caulton. It'll come out sooner or later."

# Chapter 12

Claudia Warren parked across the entrance to the O'Reilly's garden. She noted that Brian's car had been pulled out and parked on the roadside, with Frances' precious vehicle taking pride of place in the driveway. She chuckled to herself. It hadn't taken long for the widow to make some changes!

She strode up to the cottage door, a beef and Guinness pie cradled in her arms. She had made it once for an Irish Women's Brigade meeting: Frances had eaten two portions and had unbent enough to say, "Quite nice, Claudia." It was in a spare Pyrex dish, rather than a disposable one, in case she needed an excuse to call back. Claudia believed in planning ahead. She also believed in the "belt and braces" method, so she also clutched a bottle of her homemade elderberry liqueur, which contained a few extra ingredients designed to promote ease and honesty. It was a source of pride to Claudia that no one had yet withstood it.

She rang the doorbell and waited. A curtain twitched, and she glimpsed Frances O'Reilly's distinctive blonde hair. A long moment went by but eventually the door opened, and Claudia found Frances staring suspiciously out at her.

"Yes?"

"Frances! It's myself, Claudia. Claudia Warren."

"Oh. Yes, of course." She didn't look particularly pleased. Nothing daunted, Claudia pulled herself up to her full height, an impressive figure with a full bosom and an air of authority. She presented the pie solemnly.

"On behalf of the Merrion and Dun Laoghaire branch of the Irish Women's Brigade, as Brigadier General of the Leinster chapter and second in command to the Commander in Chief, I hereby present our deepest condolences on your tragic loss. Please be assured of our most sincere wishes for you at this difficult time."

A slightly bewildered Frances found the Beef and Guinness pie pressed into her hands. Taking advantage of the widow's confusion, Claudia ushered the woman into her own house with a cheery, "pop that in the oven at one hundred and eighty and it'll be piping hot in an hour!"

Just as Frances opened her mouth to object (although not as strongly as she might have, because the pie did smell mouth-wateringly delicious) Claudia rummaged in her huge bag and produced the bottle of Liqueur. "Oh, and a drop of this for your nerves..."

The other woman sniffed but conceded defeat. "Well, maybe just a drop."

She offered two glasses to Claudia who promptly filled one and half-filled the other. "I'm driving," she said, "But you should get a good dose into you, you've had a terrible shock."

Frances drank half of hers in a gulp, the warming mixture bringing a touch of colour to her long pale face. Claudia had never looked at her before; not properly. She was always annoying, or whiny or rude. If asked to describe her, Claudia would have said "tall enough, thin, neurotic - awfully moany."

83

Looking at her now, it struck her that the woman was dressed in her usual style of very expensive and colourful clothes - a well-cut lavender coloured trouser suit with an orange-patterned silk blouse. But if you looked beyond the camouflage, there were some subtle changes. Her hair looked nice and bouncy. Her face was discreetly made up, and there was overall a sort of polished air to her. Widowhood suited her.

"Sit down," Frances indicated one of the stools at the kitchen's breakfast bar, a tall, metal monstrosity which looked as uncomfortable as sitting on a bed of nettles. Claudia ignored the stool and sat herself at the kitchen table, nursing her glass of elderberry. "Sciatica," she said, "Can't manage high stools anymore. So, how are you? Is there anything we can help you with, the Brigade I mean?"

Frances was flattered despite herself. It had long been her ambition to break into the upper ranks of the Brigade, Ireland's most influential women's group. Claudia Warren was royalty to the Brigade. Her Great-grandmother had fought in the Rising and her grandmother had driven race cars across Europe. Her family was rich, and famous, two things of which Frances thoroughly approved.

"That's so kind, I do appreciate it. Although there's very little anyone can do. My poor Brian, struck down by some thug! We though Bramble Lane would such a nice, quiet place to live but I suppose nowhere is safe, these days."

Claudia tutted and nodded. "Nowhere, absolutely nowhere."

"I don't know what the Gardaí are about," Frances found herself saying. "In and out bothering me all day, but as far as I can see they haven't a clue what's happening. And I asked them to keep me updated on any developments but there hasn't been a word. I suppose they'll leave me to read it in the newspapers, like everyone else."

"How awful. I'm shocked. Here, have a tiny top up, it'll help you relax a bit. You poor thing, it sounds like a nightmare." "It *is* a nightmare. That's exactly what it is. And it turns out that cheeky young pup down the road, that Ronan Desmond, is a Garda. A detective, no less. The number of times my Brian asked him what he did for a living only to get a smart answer."

Both women tutted over the rudeness of the younger generation. "But, Frances, what on earth was poor Brian doing in that house...Kimberly cottage, was it? Are you great friends with the woman there?"

Frances bridled. "We barely knew her. I didn't know her at all. Brian went around to introduce himself, and she was very disobliging. Not our type at all. Have you seen her? Typical artist type, with messy hair and looks like she's a bit of a hippy." Claudia filed away this description to amuse the others with later, especially Eve. "It's so mysterious," she remarked.

"Mysterious?" Frances said sharply. "Nonsense. He must had seen that stupid woman's door was ajar and went to investigate. If she'd locked her door properly behind her, none of this would have happened. Careless fool." "Oh, of course. And that other woman, the teacher?"

"Oh. Margaret Furey." Frances rolled her eyes. "With her hysterics. You'd think a teacher would be able to control herself a bit better, wouldn't you? I could hear her, making a show of herself, crying and wailing. What an example for the kids she teaches."

"Hmm, but what brought her to the cottage? I read she was right there, at the scene. Isn't it a wonder they didn't arrest her?"

Frances' face darkened. "Yes, it is. I'll be surprised if they

85

don't arrest her yet."

"I suppose, being a teacher and all, they took her word for it that she wasn't involved?"

"Teacher! Hah!" the widow leaned forward and pointed a bony finger at Claudia. "I could tell you things about high and mighty Ms Furey. She might be a teacher now, but there was a time when she wasn't quite so respectable. I bet people wouldn't be half so keen on her if they knew –" Her eyes widened suddenly and she stopped herself mid sentence. "I mean, she's – she's – oh I don't know what I mean! I'm so upset, it's all been such a shock."

"Of course, and here am I keeping you talking, you must forgive me. You have a nice rest now and eat some pie when it's hot. You'll feel a lot better. You have to mind yourself." Claudia fluttered out, with lots of promises to call again, and hints that the Brigade would be delighted to see Mrs. O'Reilly at the next meeting, if she felt able. She felt quite satisfied with her visit. After all, she had gleaned two very interesting pieces of information and thanks to that very clever elixir she called her Elderberry Liqueur, the widow would have only hazy memories of a nice visit from the Brigade leadership.

Meanwhile Dymphna Moriarty had decided to tackle Margaret Furey. The young teacher was off work still, due to shock and possibly a reluctance on the school's behalf to attract a swarm of reporters. There had been quite a few on Bramble Lane the first day but as every resident firmly refused to engage with them, they had soon given up. However, if Margaret's name came to the front as a suspect, it would be very difficult for the school. "Best time to tackle her," Dymphna decided. "She's home, scared, bored and in need of a friendly face."

Armed with cakes, and some innocuous magazines – the

kind with knitting patterns and quizzes rather than gossip and crimes – she made her way down to Margaret's cottage. Despite her troubles, the girl had the garden looking perfect. It was still a riot of colour, with Chrysanthemums and Purple Cornflower, and a ground cover of Bishop's Form. Dymphna gave it a sniff of approval. Surely no one who was that good a gardener could be a murderer.

Margaret opened the door but stood on the threshold looking uncertainly at her neighbour. "I come bearing gifts," Dymphna said, "And a shoulder to cry on." Margaret responded by bursting into tears. "Oh no, no, now that's too much upset." The older woman responded as if comforting one of her young grandchildren. She patted and soothed the girl, ushered her into the living room and bustled about making tea to have with the tray of fresh baked buns. By the time the whole ritual of tea making and serving was complete, Margaret had composed herself and was looking a lot more like the capable teacher Dymphna knew.

"I'm so sorry, Mrs. Moriarty. I can't seem to stop crying. It's just – it was awful finding him, Brian, like that and then everyone seems to think I had a hand in it..." "Nonsense. Here, have one with cream on it, you need the sugar. Sugar is good for a shock, my mother always said. What was I saying? Oh yes, it's nonsense to think you killed Brian. He was an interfering, nosey man and I daresay he disturbed a burglar or something. Poking his nose in where it had no business to be."

She noted that Margaret sipped her tea and avoided eye contact.

"Unless of course, there's something you're not telling us? Oh, I'm not accusing you, dear. I'm only asking. I'm aware that to young people, women my age are just nosey old bats, but I'm not here to pry or gossip. If you would confide in me, I might be able to help you. At the very least you'd have the relief of telling someone."

The girl's soft brown eyes met the very mesmerizing eyes of her neighbour. For a moment Dymphna thought she was about to confide in her but at the last moment, she gave herself a little shake.

"I don't know what you mean. I've told the detectives everything." She looked at her watch pointedly. "Thank you so much for the tea and cakes, and I'm sorry again for getting upset."

"That's quite all right," Dymphna said. "Don't mind me, I would just hate to think of you fretting about something. I do wonder what Brian was doing though...I suppose he did just wander in. Unless he was looking for something!"

She laughed, but her eyes never left Margaret's face. She was rewarded by a slight start, and a faint reddening of the cheeks. She pressed the point just a little harder. "It's also odd about the door. Eve says she is absolutely certain she shut it firmly. But I suppose he couldn't have entered any other way. It's not like *he'd* have a key!"

"I suppose not," Margaret said faintly.

"Oh, definitely not. Maud Williams couldn't stand the man. I know she insisted on giving me a key, because he badgered her to let him have one. Some nonsense about looking after the place if she was away."

Margaret nodded politely then looked at her watch again. "I'm so sorry, Mrs. Moriarty but I absolutely must go out..." Dymphna took her leave, reasonably satisfied with the outcome. She would have to try again, but no point spooking the girl. However, she had shown more than she thought. Not a bad start, the old lady reflected.

Before returning home, Eve and her mother decided to make a detour to the estate agents and talk to Orla Moriarty. That efficient young woman, dark haired like her aunt and Grandmother, was seated behind a desk, but jumped up to greet them. Niamh she treated like a royal visitor, pressing her to sit in one of the larger padded chairs and snapping at a sulky Craig to bring coffee and biscuits, *immediately.* Eve smiled. The Old Bats had their staunch admirers.

"Now, how can I help?" She kept an eye out for her junior colleague, "I hope there's nothing wrong with Kimberly?"

"No, no, the house is perfect," Eve assured her. "But well - you know what happened there." "Of course, of course. So shocking." Orla had grey eyes, fringed by long black eyelashes. They were shrewd and bright as she studied Eve thoughtfully. "My Grandmother is up to her neck in this, isn't she?"

Niamh sniggered and Eve glared at her. "Yes, I suppose. As much as any of us. I mean, I don't know what she's said to you but we're just gathering a little information. The Gardaí are - *interested* - in both myself and Margaret Furey, because we were both there. At the scene. It's a bit uncomfortable, to be honest. So your mother and some of the other ladies -" she glanced at Niamh - "offered to "help.""

Niamh beamed complacently at the real estate agent and her daughter.

"Dear God," Orla replied, with feeling. "Yeah. That was my reaction too. In fairness though, it's nice of them to help."

"If they don't end up making it worse. Anyway, do me a favour and don't let Granny Dymphna overdo things? She's not as young as she thinks she is, if you know what I mean - she needs to be more careful."

"Don't you worry," Niamh replied. "Your Grandma knows what she's doing. We're none of us getting any younger, I'm sure, but what we lack in agility we more than make up for in life experience. It's you young ones that worry me."

"I'm fifty years old," Eve muttered.

Orla nodded sympathetically. "Do you ever wish for a normal family, Eve? One that doesn't have stubborn auld women in it?"

Eve grinned suddenly. "Actually no, if I'm honest."

Orla laughed. "I suppose I'm the same, truth be told. Okay, what have they been up to?"

Eve filled her in on the late night meeting in Orla's grandmother's kitchen and the plans they had made, finishing with the discovery of Julia O'Reilly's diary. "I'm trying to figure out why Brian was so fascinated with Kimberly Cottage. And whether it might be linked to Julia and her fiance, Constantine Farrell."

"Even if he is related to that O'Reilly family - and let's face it, it could be complete coincidence, it's a very common surname - why did he need to get into the cottage? And why did it get him killed?"

"Those are the questions that we can't answer yet. And you're right it could all be nonsense," Eve broke off as she realized Craig was standing quite close by, rooting through a filing cabinet. She waited until he gave up and moved away, before continuing quietly, "But say he was looking for something, the diary maybe. If it was that important someone else might have been looking too."

"I suppose you checked out the rest of the bookcases? Made sure Con Farrell hadn't left any other hidey-holes for his girlfriend?"

Eve blinked. "No. It never occurred to me. Oh wow, you're a genius."

"Sure, there might not be anything there. But it's worth looking."

"Yes, it is. And if you wouldn't mind looking at the previous owners for us -"

"Way ahead of you!" Orla produced a file from her drawer, and in a voice loud enough for Craig to hear, "It's the ground rent, I'm afraid. Always complicates matters with these older properties..."

Craig returned to staring at his computer.

"He's always eavesdropping," Orla said quietly, "But luckily, he's also extremely lazy and easily bored. Any hint of work to be done and he melts away. So, let's have a look here. There was only one occupier from 1909 onward, although for part of her residency the actual title deeds were in another name. Yes, here it is. Mrs. Gertrude O'Reilly moved in, with an unnamed daughter, and the title deeds were held by one William O'Reilly. Brother-in-law to the tenant. She was living rent free apart from a small fee for legal work, then in 1912 the deeds were transferred to her name and she lived there until her death in 1933. The title then passed to her daughter ...Julia, Mrs. Julia Farrell. Julia never lived there, from what I can make out. She rented it out at first, to a couple called Priory, then to another couple. The O'Sullivans. After that it was bought by the Williams." She looked up from the old documents. "Any use?"

Eve clapped her hands. "Yes, that all fits. Maud Williams wrote to Julia O'Reilly - Julia Farrell, by then. It's definitely the same Julia as the diary."

"Okay, well this may help. I found a note in the file from the time Brian bought his house, noting that "The O'Reilly's were more interested in Kimberly Cottage but despite our efforts the Williams family could not be persuaded to sell." That proves it, he was always after Kimberly." "And not for sentimental reasons, I'll bet!" Niamh crowed.

# Chapter 13

Greta Goode came from a long line of formidable women, on every side of her family tree. She had married into a quiet, well-behaved family of merchant stock, from Galway: her husband worshiped his madcap little wife, and her amiable in-laws had been tolerantly amused, airily dismissing any criticism of her as "Oh that's just Greta!" She had dragged her husband's business into the twentieth and then into the twenty-first century, insisting that they adopt new technology as well as new marketing ideas. She kept abreast of every new fashion herself, and when she handed the reins over to her children and officially retired, her first hobby was making true crime YouTube videos. Greta Goode's Gory Truths was a huge success; she branched out into other social media, but remained largely faithful to her regular viewers and new episodes of her video blog were eagerly awaited by thousands of fans.

It would be unfair to say she cackled, as she fired up her computer and settled herself down to record, but it was a close run thing. "Life in the old bat yet, eh!" She patted her hair and grinned into the web camera. "Let's see if we can't rattle some cages."

Whereas Dymphna or Niamh would tread carefully, Greta

believed in grabbing a bull by the horns. Or by anything that would hurt it and make it bellow. The first half of her show was a careful re-telling of the events in Bramble Lane, the mystery of Brian O'Reilly's presence in someone else's living room and the reaction of the Gardaí. As a proud grandmother, she included so many shots of Garda Maguire, her fans were left with the impression that the capable young woman was in sole charge of the investigation. It was an otherwise balanced presentation.

"Here's where things get murky, my dears." Greta leaned in conspiratorially. "See that great big dagger, sticking out of his back? I have it on very good authority -" she tapped her nose and winked "-that the knife does not belong to the owner of the house! It was brought there, most likely for the sole purpose of committing murder. Premeditated murder. Can any of you shed any light on the make and model? Remember the Shelton case, my pets. It was one of our eagle-eyed viewers who identified the clock as a valuable antique. That provided our detectives with the motive they needed to identify a cold blooded killer. Can you do the same again? It's quite a large and distinctive knife, so have a good look and rack your brains." "Also up for consideration, who *was* Brian? Apart from a rather nosy, rude neighbour. Any and all information gratefully received and as ever, any one who provides useful intel will get a free Greta Goode Pack - sweatshirt, hoodie and mug!"

She added, as an afterthought "And if you have any thoughts on why he was in Kimberly Cottage or you can shed light on any of the residents of Bramble Lane...let me know! Well, that's all for now but don't let me down now. Any information at all, to help solve this terrible crime!"

It might need a bit of editing, a few tweaks here and there, but she was satisfied. Greta knew her audience, her "Goode

Hunters." If there was anything to be found out, they would find it.

She showed the completed video on her channel to the rest of the ladies later that day. A hastily convened meeting saw all four of the senior ladies with Eve and Jo Maguire comparing notes in the kitchen of Kimberly Cottage. "It went live a few minutes ago and already it has five thousand views," her proud granddaughter tapped the screen on her phone. "Well done, Granny."

"It's brilliant," Eve said. "I can't believe I've never come across your videos before, Greta. I'll have to subscribe." "You did well too, you and Niamh. It looks more and more certain that Brian and Frances moved here solely to get at Kimberly Cottage. It explains the way he crept around and badgered poor Maud over the years."

"I didn't achieve as much, I'm afraid," Dymphna said. "However, I didn't want to push too hard in case she just clammed up. Margaret is definitely hiding something and I'm sure it's the missing clue as to why he was in this house. And how he got in. A thought crossed my mind talking to her, and I'm not sure if it's just my suspicious mind."

"Go on, you can't say that and not tell us!"

"This is pure guesswork, you understand. But when I mentioned keys, and how Brian got into the house, she went awfully quiet. Maud Williams gave me a full set for emergencies, but you remember during the Covid lockdown, how everyone our age was afraid to go shopping? I remember Margaret doing a lot of errands for Maud. She usually left the shopping on the doorstep for her, but occasionally she carried it in. In fact, I'm almost sure she let herself in on occasion. I thought nothing of it at the time, and didn't pay a lot of attention but..."

"What if she had a latch key?" Eva stared at her. "I didn't bother locking the five-lever lock, I just pulled the door behind me. Anyone with a latch key could have entered."

"Precisely."

"You need to get it out of her, Dymphna," Niamh's voice held a note of urgency. "We can't be sure the Gardaí have ruled out Eve and if we can't show how he got in…"

"It's okay, Mam! Jennie thinks they're satisfied I had nothing to do with it." Jo Maguire coughed discreetly. All eyes turned to her as she murmured, "It might not be that simple."

"It's not?"

"Well, I agree you're bottom of the suspect list but right now, there's only two names on that list. If we could show that Margaret had a key to the door, it would help eliminate you."

Eve nodded. It was all very reasonable, but it still made her stomach knot. She wanted to feel safe but not by throwing another person under the bus, as it were.

"I appreciate you being open with us, Jo." " It'll be grand. Don't worry too much, we're not bumbling eejits like you see in the movies. We'll get to the bottom of it. Claudia, how did it go with the grieving widow?"

Claudia was bursting with her news. "I had a very interesting conversation with Frances O'Reilly. She wasn't a bit happy to see me, but she was flattered by the mention of the Brigade. I hinted broadly that she would have a shot at the committee and plied her with my elderberry liqueur." Five heads nodded appreciatively. "She didn't mean to but she told me two interesting things…the first was that she and Brian know something about Margaret, something about her past. It's something that if it came out, could affect her job in St. Malachy's and her reputation as a teacher." "And the second thing?" "That she was present at the crime scene, even though she was supposed to be miles away."

A stunned silence greeted this revelation, and Claudia basked in it.

"How on earth do you know that!"

"Because after a glass and a half of my elixir, she let slip that she could, and I quote, *"hear her, making a show of herself!"* Well, I don't care how acute your hearing is, you couldn't hear that from the Merrion Complex, could you? She must have been here, on Bramble Lane."

"Are you absolutely sure she didn't say she heard *about* her, not she heard her?"

"One hundred percent" Claudia huffed. "I tell you, she said she heard it herself."

"Then that is a brilliant piece of detection, Madam Brigadier!" Eve mock saluted her, while the others gave an enthusiastic round of applause.

"Excellent work, Claudia," Dymphna said. "Now, what do we do with this information?"

"Pass it on to Ronan Desmond!" Eve said firmly. "That's something he needs to know, and the same goes for any other concrete pieces of information we get."

"And what do I say, exactly? I fed Frances O'Reilly a potion to loosen her tongue and now I know she was at the crime scene?" Claudia rolled her eyes and her three friends all chuckled. Eve sighed. It was a bit like herding cats, or managing a room of toddlers, dealing with these feisty seniors.

"No. You tell him, casually, that you were talking to her, and she let slip something odd. Say you thought it was probably nothing but you felt you should pass it on, because you under-

97

stood that she was in work at the time of the murder. You make it sound natural, and you don't let on that we've been snooping behind his back."

"Fine. I can do that. Although I still think we should keep it to ourselves for now, maybe catch her out in a lie or two."

"I'll do it," Jo volunteered. "I'll say you were bending my ear asking after Granny and you mentioned it."

"I dunno," Niamh had a mutinous look that her daughter recognized. "Are we not better off waiting until we have more concrete evidence? What if Ronan Desmond throws a hissy fit and bans us from snooping around?"

"We tell the Detectives," Eve said firmly. To her surprise Granny Goode came to her defense.

"She's right, ladies. I pass any information received from the public on to the Force. Well, I tell Jo here, but it's the same thing. If I didn't and it came out later, they'd blame her for a start – they'd never believe her granny didn't keep her informed. And it's not about getting the credit, it's about solving the crime. The Gardaí have the resources to follow up on things. They have the power to arrest someone. We have the ability to ferret out information. See how it works?"

The other ladies nodded solemnly, even Niamh. Eve could see that for all her flightiness, Granny Goode was respected by her peers. "Thanks, Greta. Which leads us to – what do we need to do next?"

"I think Dymphna is right," Niamh said, "She needs to tread carefully with Margaret, no point in crowding her. Maybe give it a day. The most urgent thing seems to me to follow up on Julia Farrell and try to figure out what the connection is between her and the present day O'Reilly's."

"Orla asked if we had checked to see were there any other

hiding places in the cottage. She thought if Con had gone to the trouble of making one place, he may well have created another. It makes sense, if they were married she may have needed somewhere to hide her rings and marriage certificate. She probably took them when she left but maybe there's something else left behind."

"I'll check that," Jo volunteered, "If Eve doesn't mind me poking around, that is. I'm good at searches." "A professional eye would be great, thanks," Eve agreed. "As for myself, I would like to see if we can trace the Farrell family, maybe a descendant can help us." "Start online," Claudia advised. "I'm going to find out everything I can about Frances. There's a Brigade committee meeting this afternoon, I'll start there."

Dymphna and Niamh volunteered to visit Frances' boutique and pump the sales assistants, see if they could confirm her absence on the day of the murder. "We could also follow up on anything Greta's followers turn up."

"Oh that reminds me, I haven't checked..." Greta produced her phone and opened the App. She started to scroll through comments, muttering under her breath as she did so. "No, that's ridiculous... hmm, interesting...no, no, possibly...AHA!" She looked up and said triumphantly, "Pay dirt, Ladies! Listen to this. It's a private message. "

"*Greta, I'm such a major fan. I can't believe I finally have some information to help in one of your investigations. I was watching the news and they showed the house, with people in front of it. The man who found the two women standing over that poor man, that's Tom MacDonagh. I know him, from the local Drama Society. And then I recognized the victim, Brian O'Reilly. I saw him, arguing with MacDonagh last Monday – two days before the murder! And they were screaming at each other, it wasn't a little argument. At first I couldn't make out the words from where I was, they were standing at the corner of Bramble lane and Merrion Avenue. But as I walked closer, I did hear MacDonagh call him a low-life, and O'Reilly responded by saying he would wipe the smile off MacDonagh's face. He also said something along the lines of "You'll regret this, I'll make sure of it" and MacDonagh muttered, "Not if I get to you first.""*

"Oh, good grief...not Tom!" Dymphna looked upset. "He's such a good person, I can't believe he'd kill anyone."

Eve shared her view. She had only met him briefly, but he certainly seemed like a kind, thoughtful man. Anyone was capable of violence, in a moment of madness, she supposed. But could a man who seemed so genuinely kind, whom her shrewd neighbour liked so much, stand by and watch Margaret and Eve be accused unjustly? Comfort Margaret, who was having hysterics with fear and shock...knowing he was to blame? It was a level of hypocrisy that would be chilling.

But, she thought glumly, I thought Peter would never cheat on me. I'm no judge of character.

"I think it's unlikely, but we need to follow it up. Dymphna, you know him best so you should go have a chat. Tell him what we've been told and hear his explanation. "

"And do we tell *this* to Detective Desmond?" Everyone looked at Granny Goode. She cocked her head, reminding Eve of an inquisitive robin.

"I don't know," Eve admitted. "Jo? "

"I say hold off, for the moment. That's off the record, obviously. But I know Tom, he's sound. Have a chat first, before you land him in it. I'll pass on the information once we have a clearer picture of what they were fighting about, or if it was as dramatic as all that. For all we know, this is someone who has a grudge, or maybe Tom stole the lead role from them in the Drama society. Let's just double check the facts first."

"Okay!" Eve was ridiculously relieved. After all, she hardly knew the man. It shouldn't matter if he turned out to be a suspect. She should be worrying about her herself. But he had made a good impression, there was no denying it. It would be a pity if it was misleading.

Pushing the thought firmly to the back of her mind, she pushed on. "We'll see what tomorrow brings. Good work all round, ladies. You're all amazing."

She drifted off to sleep that night feeling a lot better about things. It might seem silly to outsiders but the fact that the elder ladies, the wise women she remembered from her youth, were on her side was comforting. During her marriage, she had let slip any pretense of being like them. Eve had never felt like she had serious talent in that direction, it was Conor who was sensitive and intuitive while she had always been practical and -well, mundane. Peter had been sarcastic about her own occasional flashes of intuition, and absolutely dismissive of any attempt to explain her mother's abilities, to the point of calling Niamh delusional. Her confidence eroded by his scorn, Eve had stopped trying to explain and soon began to ignore the topic herself, even among family. In fact, she recalled with shame, she had been quite hard on her mother, constantly shutting Niamh down when she made any reference to the old ways, or to anything that touched on the magical. It must have hurt her feelings. But the moment she needed help, the way these women made themselves useful, got involved, touched her.

The next morning, refreshed by a deep sleep, Eve munched her way through some toast, musing about the latest developments. Tom MacDonagh had impressed her on the day, she admitted it to herself. But she barely knew him and Dymphna, while a good judge of character, was not infallible either. He had a terrible argument with Brian, shortly before the murder and he had arrived on the scene very quickly.

And Frances O'Reilly was present, close enough to hear poor Margaret having hysterics. Eve cast her mind back. Margaret's sobbing had been largely contained until they exited the house, into the front garden. That was when she had properly broken down. If Frances had been present and had heard her clearly enough to describe to Claudia, then she had to be on Bramble lane, probably only a door or two away. Hiding maybe, in one of the neighbour's driveways...or her own. Only Brian's car had been parked in the driveway when Eve had strolled around the lane. But the Merrion Complex was so near at hand, any reasonably mobile person would be over and back in under fifteen minutes.

At least the detectives would now have two more suspects, even if one of them was Tom. It took some of the pressure off Margaret - and Eve. Jo had volunteered to call around in the afternoon for a thorough search of the cottage. The morning she would spend online, chasing the Farrell connection. Julia Farrell, nee O'Reilly, was around twenty in 1912, and would be long gone by now. But in her seventies, she was living in the address Maud Williams wrote to, and it was just possible there were still family members living there. Eve read it again - Keeltigan, Gortmalogue, County Tipperary. She typed it into Google and up popped a list of townlands in the county, with the additional information that it was in a area with the unlikely name of "*Iffa and Offa,*" one of the ancient Baronies of Tipperary. She tried the eircode finder, a handy website which pinpointed the unique postal code of every building in

Ireland. It took a few tries but at last a post code popped up. The next step was to input the eircode into a maps App on her smartphone, and cross her fingers - and yes! Eve zoomed in as far as possible, opting for the "street view" so she could see footage of the house.

It was a large house, Victorian at a guess, with extensive gardens. Like many Irish country houses from that era, it had an imposing, grey front with large evenly spaced windows and a porch with columns on either side. There was a wide gravel-covered drive, and well kept hedgerows around the property. It looked as if there was a large rear garden, and a large freestanding garage. Eve felt a surge of pride for Julia and Constantine. It seemed the intrepid young couple had found success at least. She glanced at the journal, in pride of place on her desk and back at the screen.

"I hope it was a happy life, Julia," she thought. "I suppose we are about to find out!"

# Chapter 14

Once she had the phone number for the Farrell family's old address, Eve had to steel herself to ring. She far preferred text or email, but time was pressing. They simply couldn't wait for someone to read an email, and respond at their leisure. Taking a couple of deep breaths and feeling a little foolish, she dialed the number and crossed her fingers.

It was answered on the fifth ring, by a childish voice.

"Hi?" it inquired, "Is that Nana?"

Eve laughed. "No, pet. This isn't your Nana. Are your parents there, please?"

"I'm waiting for my Nana to ring," the youngster replied. "Who dis?"

"I'm Eve. I'm trying to get hold of your mammy or daddy, can you put them on?"

"No. Are you a friend of my Mammy's? Do you know my Nana?"

"I'm sorry, I don't know her."

"That's weird. Everyone knows my Nana."

"I'm sure they do love. Listen, could you do me a favour? could you call for your parents?"

"I have a red bike. It's faster than Molly's."

Eve groaned. There was nothing as single-minded as a small

child and no living creature harder to persuade.

"Okay, pet, that sounds lovely. Tell you what, I'll ring back later -"

"Here's my Mammy. MAMMY!" the child screamed at ear splitting volume. Eve winced and held the phone away from her ear. "There's a lady on the phone. She doesn't know my Nana."

"Go on with you," She could hear someone ushering the kid away at the other end of the line. "Honestly, Con, you're a divil!"

"Con!" Eve exclaimed. "Hello?" the voice was pleasant if a little wary, with a Tipperary accent. "Yes, that was Con. My son. Who is this?"

"Oh hello, my name is Eve Caulton. I live in a place called Kimberly Cottage, in Dublin. I don't know if you know it, but I think it used to belong to Julie Farrell. Her original name was O'Reilly, and she would have lived here around nineteen eleven or nineteen twelve..." "Julia? Julia was my husband's grandmother. Wait a moment, I think you should be talking to him." There was a brief pause, followed by a murmured exchange. The woman's voice was replaced by a male, the same accent and the same pleasant, friendly tone.

"Hello. Seamus Farrell here. How can I help you?"

Eve repeated her introduction, adding "I know this is out of the blue but I found a diary belonging to Julia. It dates from the time she first married Constantine Farrell, Dr. Farrell. He was a poor medical student, and she was living with her mother..."

"Oh, my goodness, seriously?" He repeated what she had said, and she heard his wife exclaiming in surprise. "A diary? Well, we are most interested. My grandmother was a remark-able woman, and she led a very interesting life but the one thing

105

she rarely talked about was her life in Dublin, and her mother. My father and his siblings were never allowed to meet their grandmother, and Con, their father, told them to let it be, that it was very painful for Julia."

"So she never told you about that period?" Eve felt a pang of disappointment. She had hoped to hear the missing part of the story from Julia's descendants.

"Well now, that's where you're wrong. As a young boy, I used to spend a lot of time with Granny Julia. She told me stories she didn't tell anyone else, about her own father and her early life. She was brought up in a very affluent family at first, then her father died. It turned out he was up to his eyes in debt, left her mother and her penniless." "The diary mentions some of that," Eve replied.

"Ah great!"

"But it ends when Julia tells her mother about her marriage to Con, and all hell breaks loose."

"Oh, I'd love to read it," Seamus said. "She glossed over all of that." "Look, the moment I can I'll turn over Julia's diary to you, it belongs to you in fairness." Eve recounted the story of finding the journal, as quickly as possible. "But it's the murder that concerns me at the moment. I'm sorry to say, but I think Brian O'Reilly was a cousin of yours. Distant but all the same..."

"There was no love lost with that side of the family," Seamus assured her. "Don't be worrying about that. Obviously, it's terrible the man was killed but my mother severed ties with them all. And for good reason. How about this? I'll nip into the study and fire off an email to you. I wrote down all the stories my grandparents told me, it's a bit of a personal project. I'm thinking of doing a family history book, for my kids and my sister's children. I'll send you on "Julia's Story" and it should fill you in on the bits you're missing. You send me the diary when you can, and anything else about her life in Kimberly Cottage, her mother, her Uncle William...you'll see why when you read her story!"

Eve sent a silent prayer of thanks down the line. "Seamus Farrell, you're a gentleman and from what I read, you're like your Grandparents. I'd say they'd be fierce proud of you. And I take it that little man I spoke to is Con, after Constantine."

"He is. He's Constantine, and my sister is Constance. My father was Seamus, after his grandfather, Con's father who worked so hard to put him through college. My uncles were named Jules, for Julia and Patrick, for Julia's father. And my Aunt is Nora, for Con's mother. Julia's parents-in-law became her second parents. They moved with them to Tipperary and lived with them helping with the children while my grandfather built up his practice. Good people."

"And did any of you become Doctors like Con?"

"One in each generation," Seamus replied proudly. "So, I'm talking to the third Dr. Farrell?"

"No, no, not me! I'm a software engineer. Dr. Farrell is my sister. Julia would have loved that."

Eve smiled broadly. "I'm so glad, and I can't wait to read what happened to Julia and Con. I'll be waiting for that email!"

Seamus promised faithfully she wouldn't have to wait long, and ended the call with an invitation to deliver the diary in person, once it was no longer needed. A shaft of sunlight came through the cottage windows and fell on her shoulder, as she waited for the email to arrive. It felt like a warm presence and Eve was reminded of Dymphna's comment about Julia wanting her to find the diary.

"I'm doing my best to figure it all out," she said aloud. "Your family seem nice - you did well, you and Con."

In response, her computer pinged, and a fresh email popped up. *SeamusFarrell@irelandmail dot com.*

She opened it and read,

"*Dear Eve,*

*Again, delighted you contacted us. Hope you enjoy the attached file, it's pretty much the story as told to me by the woman herself. Keep in touch, and remember you've promised to come down and meet us all!*"

Eve clicked the attachment and began to read.


By the time Jo Maguire arrived, clutching her lunch in one hand and a huge coffee cup in the other, Eve was dancing with excitement. "I've been bursting to tell someone, Jo, but I need to wait til we're all together. But seeing as you're a fine upstanding member of the Force and you can be trusted to keep a secret..."

"Don't!" Jo held up her hand. "I can't lie, not to Mrs. Moriarty and my Granny. She'd know, before I even sat down. Keep your secret and let me eat my lunch. I'm going to search every inch of this place, and I need no distractions."

"Spoilsport. I suppose I will have to wait then. Everyone's meeting here at seven o'clock, so be prepared for major revelations. And search - search everywhere, search like you're looking for a ton of illicit substances and cache of arms."

"Where will you be while I'm rifling through your belongings?"

"I am going to the Probate Office in town, I've an appointment to look at some public records." She laughed at Jo's astounded face. "Hah! Now you're sorry. You should have taken me up on my offer to spill the beans. Now you can wait til the rest of them are here."

Jo laughed but stuck to her guns. After a hurried lunch, she put on close-fitting gloves and carefully, methodically set about her task. It was no easy feat, removing books and ornaments, checking drawers and cabinets, even measuring to check for hidden areas. She worked her way through the bookshelves, across the living room and into the old-fashioned scullery. Twice she found something, paused for a long time to move and catalogue her finds. She took a break, to sit thoughtfully and consider the results of the search to that point. Then she resumed, checking floorboards and even the steps on the staircase. In the end, she stood in the middle of the living room with her hands on her hips and a satisfied smile. Eve wouldn't be the only one with a story to tell later.

While Jo was hard at work on her painstaking task, Dymphna had decided to tackle Tom MacDonagh. The weather still being fine, she knew he would be hard at work in his garden. There was no sign of him out front but a small pathway at the side of Rowan Tree Cottage lead to the back garden. She made her way along this, and found Tom on his knees, tending to a row of tomato plants, already heavy with fruit.

"That's a great display, Tom. You've quite a knack with fruit and veg."

"Hello! Thanks, yes, I'm very pleased. I've a load of lettuce too if you fancy any? last of the year, I think. And I'll have more blueberries soon."

"I'll take them if you can spare them. But, Tom, I'm not here to talk about fruit." He looked at her, surprised at her serious tone.

"Is something wrong?" He sounded anxious.

"I don't know. Someone told me something, and I don't know

how true it is. I wanted to ask you first rather than say anything behind your back." "That sounds very mysterious," He stood up quickly, a very agile man for his age. She watched as he removed his gardening gloves and walked across to the patio table. It was disconcerting to be reminded that beneath his mild manners, he was a tall, strong man. He was also fit. In fact, although it was unlikely, fit enough to get over the back wall of Kimberly Cottage and leg it down that tiny back track that ran the length of the gardens. Through his own back garden and then stroll out the front door, to be seen entering the cottage through the front door...in time to discover Eve and Margaret.

She shivered as the sun suddenly disappeared behind a cloud.

"Dymphna?" Tom pointed to a chair at the table. "Sit yourself down and tell me what's bothering you. I'll make tea."

"No tea for me, thanks. I'm going around to Eve's shortly, her Mam is coming over. We're going shopping." She preferred if he knew she was expected somewhere and would be missed.

"Okay. So, what's bothering you?"

"Someone has approached Greta to say they saw you having a terrible row with Brian a few days before the murder." She watched his face closely. "They said they overheard you threatening him."

If she was expecting any kind of reaction, it was either rage or fear. Instead, he threw his head back and laughed.

"I bet they did. I can't remember exactly what I said but I'm fairly sure it's unrepeatable in polite society. And I distinctly remember telling him he'd get his, or similar. He was as bad, in my defense. And he said he'd get me, I think he even shook his fist at me." A grin spread across his face. "We were, in short, two ridiculous, middle-aged men making utter fools of ourselves."

Dymphna remained unconvinced. "I'm sorry, Tom but we have to know, what on earth were you arguing about?"

For a moment, she thought he would refuse to answer. His expression remained pleasant and open, but there was a tightening of the jaw and a tiny clench of his fists. She sensed rather than heard the sharpness of his breath. Then it passed and he sighed.

"I'm embarrassed, if you must know. I let Brian get under my skin and I'm ashamed to say it, but I was as close to punching him on the nose...well, it was a close-run thing. It wasn't just one thing, you see. He had a bee in his bonnet about young Margaret. Constantly making snide comments about her. Sometimes more than snide, if you follow me. Downright nasty. Then he began to pick on her garden - you know her wildflowers for the pollinators and so on. Calling it messy and a disgrace and saying we should all complain. Every time I set eyes on the man, he started on about it. I laughed it off, and just avoided him but it grated on my nerves. And I'm sure you must have noticed, it got to that girl, affected her. She was nervous around him, it was clear he was bullying her."

"On the day we argued, I bumped into him on my morning walk and of course he started up on his hobby horse again. I'd had quite enough of it, so I told him off. Said he should be ashamed of himself and that her garden was an example to us all. And that I planned on starting one myself." He couldn't suppress a grin. "I may also have said I was going to lobby the residents next spring to agree to delayed mowing, let the dandelions and so on bloom to help the bees. I thought his head would explode! He had a complete temper tantrum, which was grand until he...well, he made a remark about how much I "liked" Margaret, how I must be getting something in return."

Tom's cheeks went pink recalling the exchange. "I absolutely lost my temper then. It was a disgusting suggestion, I'm more than old enough to be her father."

"Grandfather, in fact," Dymphna said, straight-faced.

"Ah steady on, I'm only 60 you know. Let's stick with father! Anyway, it was a nasty thing to say and that man had a dirty mind. But it was all in his head, you know. Once I calmed down I was able to laugh it off, because there was absolutely nothing in it. I let it go. Honestly, it had nothing to do with the murder."

"Does Ronan know about the argument?"

Tom's eyes twinkled at her. "You did consider me a suspect, didn't you? I mentioned to him that I had an altercation, yes. I -I didn't mention his comments about Margaret. That may seem wrong to you -"

"But you didn't want to add more motive to her," Dymphna finished for him. "It's okay. I totally get it. Same reason we didn't tell Ronan about your argument, we didn't want to give him a reason to suspect you unfairly."

Tom eyed her curiously. "Thank you. May I inquire...who are this "we" you keep mentioning?"

Dymphna considered him carefully, then made a decision. "I've quite a long story for you. And if you make that cup of tea now, I wouldn't say no."

# Chapter 15

The two detectives were feeling discouraged. A painstaking search of the scrub and bushes at the back of Bramble Lane had so far yielded nothing much of interest beyond some fragments here and there, material and paper and other bits that might or might not prove relevant.

"Probably none of it will be remotely connected," Detective Cullen remarked sourly, as Detective Desmond watched their team work their way slowly through the overgrown shrubs and briars.

"You can see why it's called Bramble Lane, though," Ronan remarked, as he plucked bits of Blackberry bushes from his hair and examined the tiny thorn scratches on his hands. "I wore gloves, and those brambles just shredded them.

"Nice place to live," Cullen eyed the cottages and their gardens appreciatively, "But awfully quiet. When there's no one getting murdered, obviously."

Ronan ignored him and continued to watch the searchers.

"Over here!" The call went up from one of the young, uni-formed Gardaí. Both detectives moved at once, their weariness replaced instantly with alertness and hope. The Garda extended her hand and pointed towards a thicket of especially dense bramble. "There, about halfway down."

An object, inexpertly wrapped in a white plastic bag was just visible, stuck into the bush about halfway down from eye-level. It had been wrapped but not sealed and had opened enough for a distinctive black handle to be recognizable.

"That looks like -"

"Yes. The same handle as the murder weapon."

"Well done," Cullen said approvingly. The Garda grinned and tried to look nonchalant. "Good work. Now hand me an evidence bag and if you had secateurs handy that'd be a blessing." To his surprise, she produced a sturdy pair of gardening secateurs and an evidence bag. "What's your name? Doyle? Excellent." Cullen was known for being sparse with praise, but in his eyes, any cop who had the sense to equip themselves with useful, non-regulation items during a search deserved a commendation. He made a mental note of her name, and pushed on. Using the sharp scissors, he snipped away gently until the bag with its contents could be removed with the minimum disturbance. He then slipped it out and into the evidence bag in one expert movement.

Straightening up, he smiled at Ronan. "Now, this - *this* is interesting."

Half an hour later, Jo Maguire listened intently as her colleague, Una Doyle whispered the news to her. "I swear, Jo, he asked my name and said "Excellent!" I nearly fell over."

"Good for you, girl. I'm delighted. I told you, keep plugging away and it'll happen. Cullen's not the worst by any means and he'll remember a good job. But are you sure, it's the same kind of knife as the murder weapon?"

"Oh absolutely. You couldn't mistake that handle."

Jo mulled it over, wondering what her granny would think of this new development. If the murder weapon had been missing, it would be a simple case of having found it. But they had the murder weapon, it had never left Brian O'Reilly's back. There was no question of that, Forensics had been clear. So now they had the match of it, hidden along what they presumed could be the killer's escape route, but why have two identical weapons?

She shook her head. Now wasn't the time to try figure this out, she had a lot on hand this shift. Slipping out her phone, she opened her message app and chose "G.G. and friends." G.G. was of course her Granny Goode, and the friends were the mad yokes she hung around with.

"*News,*" she typed. "*Match of knife used on B found in waste land behind BL.*"

Immediately, messages crossed as the ladies replied. Honestly, they were worse than teenagers, never letting their phones out of their hands. Jo had read a book recently where a woman in her late fifties was described as "scared of technology" which bewildered her. Anyone she knew that age either still worked, and used computers or computerized systems, or had a smart phone that they used constantly. Her granny must have broken the speed of light in replying, so quickly did her response appear.

"*Forensics? Can't be sure is clean yet. But very odd, why 2 identical?*"

Eve Caulton contributed, "*Can see search from my back bedroom, they're finishing up.*"

Niamh supplied, "*Two weapons, maybe sold in pairs? Antiques? Tom would know.*"

"Genius!" thought Jo and went in search of Detective Desmond. "Sir? Maybe both were sold together, like a pair. If they're antiques, perhaps a dealer would recognize them. Tom MacDonagh is a retired Auctioneer, and an expert in Antiques."

"You think he might own them?" Cullen sat upright, for all the world like a terrier catching a scent.

"No!" Jo cursed herself. She hadn't meant to spread suspicion to Tom. "I meant more like, he might be able to identify them or at least confirm if they're common or antique and so on."

"Hmm." Cullen thought for a moment. "It's a good idea, but I think we need to use an expert who isn't involved in the case. And we should search the cottages on Bramble Lane, see if anyone has a set of these."

Jo acknowledged he was right. Much as she trusted Tom, obviously the detectives couldn't be sure of his innocence, and showing a suspect or even a witness sensitive evidence might not be best practice. "I get it. Still, worth checking out with an independent source?"

"It is, and good work."

Duty done, she went back to her work but first fired off one more message to the ladies.

"They'll check it. Not with Tom but will check." They'd have to be satisfied with that.

Detective Desmond was far from satisfied, though. It was another complication in a very odd case.

"So we have a killer who may or may not have come in through a back door which may have been left unlocked by the owner, or not. We have a victim, who may or may not have used the back door to enter or may have had keys, but we can't find them. The victim is unknown to the house owner beyond the merest acquaintance but everyone else on the scene knows him well, as a neighbour. We've a murder weapon, that has an identical twin and the first was left in the body while the innocent match was well hidden."

"That's about the shape of it," Cullen agreed. "I hate this case."

It may have depressed the official detectives but the news about a spare weapon galvanized the unofficial investigators into action. This was where Greta came into her own, with her army of devoted listeners. She had long ago created subgroups of useful contacts, including experts on all manner of interesting things. Her ability to inspire devoted loyalty ensured that once Granny Goode asked a favour, it was as good as done.

For her video appeal, she'd used a photo published online, good enough for a general appeal, but not detailed enough for an expert eye. It was entirely possible she could get her hands on a clearer, official photo, but for several reasons, not least that it would be difficult to explain *how* she had an official photo of a murder weapon, she decided to use an alternative.

"*Eve, can you draw a sketch of the knife handle? and send it to me.*"

Eve drew as carefully detailed an image as she could and attached it to a message. Greta chose from her list of contacts and sent a cryptic message to a well known art dealer, a young man who owed his job to the Greta Goode true crime groupies, and their ability to track people down. He had come away from the experience wiser – never again would he accept a personal cheque in payment for a valuable art piece – and grateful. He was only too happy to examine the sketch and make some inquiries.

Within the hour, long before the Gardaí received the same information from their own choice of expert, Greta had learned and shared the news. The handles were almost certainly from a paired set, Edwardian period, used to carve large birds like

Turkey or Goose, and while not very rare, were not commonly found either. They would be sold in a pair, possibly with a large fork of similar design.

"I'm not sure what it means," she admitted, "but whoever owned them, would have had a matching pair. Maybe discarded the spare, so it didn't draw attention?"

The two detectives on the case were thinking along the same lines.

"Too dangerous to leave the spare lying around, it would be noticed. But why discard it there? Wouldn't it be much easier to drive to a lake and toss it in?"

"Depends on time," Ronan said. "Or there's something we're not seeing. Yet."

# Chapter 16

Claudine smiled and nodded as the women around her chattered but her mind was elsewhere. Committee meetings were a mix of socializing and work; there were quite a few events coming up, many for the first time since the pandemic had seen everything canceled. There were new rules to navigate, and the difficulty of attracting people back, after a two year break. All very difficult. She was also aware that she had a limited amount of time to get hold of the women she thought might have information on Frances O'Reilly. One of them was passing by at that precise moment, clutching a tray of iced buns and looking hassled. "Excuse me," Claudia took the opportunity to move away from her group and follow Pam Nolan. "Pam! Let me help you there." "Oh, thank you, Brigadier - such a nuisance, whoever used the kitchen area last left it in a terrible state. We're behind with refreshments, I'm afraid."

"Never mind, it's just us committee members today,"Claudia comforted her, "And I'll have a chat with the caretaker, make sure an eye is kept on cleaning up."

The Irish Women's Brigade Hall was often rented out to other groups, some less reliable than others. But it was a valuable source of revenue for the Brigade so they took the rough with the smooth. Claudia followed Pam into the kitchen, helped get things in order and soon had a respectable array of treats ready for after the meeting. "We'll be starting in a few minutes," she said, "All we have to do is make the tea and coffee, and that won't hold us up long."

"Thanks," Pam said with feeling, "It's impossible to get some of these women to pitch in, you'd think the catering volunteers were the hired help."

"And that's another item to put on this meeting's agenda. A room full of capable women, you'd think they wouldn't stand around with their arms swinging watching a few of their comrades struggle." The Brigade had its roots in the proud struggle for Independence and Claudia thought it was high time some of the newer members remembered that. Just a hundred years earlier, Brigadier would have been a rank rather than an honorific. These elegant socialites would have been laughed out the door.

"While I have you, Pam, I wanted to ask you something. It's not just idle gossip, I promise. But am I right in thinking you were acquainted with that man who was murdered near here? In one of those cottages up Bramble Lane?"

"Oh my heavens, yes. Well...when I say acquainted, I had met him." Pam looked around to make sure no one would overhear and dropped her voice to a near whisper. "You should never speak ill of the dead, I know, but my God, he was a terrible human being. I'm not a bit surprised he met a sticky end."

"No one seems to be surprised at that. How did you meet him?"

"Socially at first, but you know I work in the Merrion Private?" Pam was an administrator in a local, private hospital. "Brian came into the clinic there, with a sore wrist. There was a small queue, nothing much, but when I tried to check him in, he kicked up a terrible stink. Said he would have gone to A&E if he wanted to wait to be seen. Like, he'd have been four hours or more in the local emergency room, not five minutes in the Merrion Private, but there you are. Entitled, selfish man. I calmed him down, told him to wait to be called and thought that was an end to it."

"About ten minutes later, a kid was rushed in - a little kid, like six or seven. Broken arm, horrible break and obviously in agony. Doctor Azuri rushed out when she heard him screaming, and of course took him in first. Poor little mite, everyone was full of sympathy. Except Brian. He kicked up another huge fuss about the child "queue jumping." He was quite ridiculous, but he caused so much trouble we had to fit him in next. Then his wife came to pick him up, and she was as bad. Thoroughly unpleasant couple. She kept giving out to him for hurting his arm - something about climbing over a wall - while he gave out to us for everything we said or did. Nightmare."

"Wow. I don't suppose you ever saw him again."

"Oh I most certainly did. He insisted on a follow up consultation with the doctor, but refused to pay for it. It took me almost four months of continually chasing him up to get the payment."

Claudia clucked in sympathy. "I had heard he was difficult. I know Frances, of course. She's in the junior section - one of these part-timers who like to turn up to social events but don't do any work."

"Oh, I've seen her, now that you mention it. You know who would know her well? Liza Dunne. She's very much a part-timer too, and if I recall correctly, she and Frances were on the sub-committee for last Easter's dance. Don't you remember Sahana Puri telling us they left everything to that poor sap

Philomena and swanned around giving orders?" "Of course! I knew there was some reason we all thought she was poison."

"Go ask Sahana, and after that try Liza, if you can get a sensible word out of her. You should talk to Liza anyway. She would know a lot about that case."

"Would she?" Claudia had a feeling she should know the answer but for the life of her, she couldn't think why the flighty, vapid Liza would be connected to Eve Caulton and Kimberly - "Oh!"

"Penny drop?" Pam grinned at her. "Liza Dunne is married to the ex-husband of that unfortunate woman. The one in whose living room they found the body."

"Eve. Eve Caulton. Liza Dunne is her husband's new wife" Claudia groaned. "Oh dear!"

"You know the first wife?"

"Yes, she's my friend's daughter. Oh well, can't be helped, can it? Thank you, Pam, you've been a great help."

For the next hour, the Brigadier turned her attention to the business of the Brigade. She delivered a pointed speech about the behaviour expected from members, and that if anyone thought it was okay to leave anything to a handful of active members, they knew where the door was. The catering volunteers were inundated with offers of help to clear up.

Her job done; Claudia cornered Sahana. The two women were old pals, and Sahana was happy to have a comfortable gossip about Frances O'Reilly.

"Oh my goodness, do I know her? She's the bane of my existence, Claudia." Sahana spoke with feeling. "I could strangle that woman, truly I could. Frankly if she'd been the one murdered, I wouldn't have been a bit surprised. Always "flashing the cash" as my kids say. Boasting about where she went on holiday, how much her car cost, childish stuff. No interest in history, not a bit charitable. I have no idea why she joined the brigade, to be frank."

"Social climbing," Claudia said shortly. "Some of these women think it's all about networking and making connections."

"They don't know how to be of use," Sahana smiled at her friend. "I suppose it takes all sorts, you can't expect everyone to be *wise*."

They exchanged a knowing look, and Claudia replied, "Doesn't stop them being as annoying as a wasp in a jam factory, though."

There was a distinct hint of cackle about their laughter at that one. Claudia thought of another question.

"Do you know anything about where the O'Reilly's used to live, where they came from? They were very nosy about everyone else, but it appears no one seems to know much about them."

"As it happens, I do know a little." Sahana replied. "Frances and I have a few acquaintances in common, not that she realizes it. My friend Anita owns a boutique in the city centre. Frances used to work there, and oh my word! does Anita have some stories to tell. She always wondered why Frances wanted to work there, because she was clearly *not* in need of a few bob. Thought maybe the husband was a bit mean with money, or that she was bored. Everything was fine at first, though. Frances worked hard, seemed friendly and pleasant. She was interested in the business, always asking questions. After a bit, Anita found it grating. Frances was always prying - looking at invoices, taking notes, odd stuff she simply had no reason to know. Anita gets a lot of her stock from an uncle in Jaipur, but the accessories and some of the top end pieces come from Irish designers. Handmade, unique stuff." "One day, one of the designers contacted Anita. She makes unique head pieces, a bestseller for Anita's shop. She said that Frances had contacted her. Offered her a contract to make exclusively for Frances' boutiques in the Merrion and around the country. Four in total. Now, this girl owes everything to Anita, who worked tirelessly to promote her designs and gave her a start in the business. So, she had no intention of doing the dirty on her, but she led Frances on. Frances told her she and her husband own a lot of property, and that she could even get her a design space in Dublin or Kilkenny at a low cost. She let slip that they were originally from Kilkenny, and that they were connected to some big house there. Very posh family, by all accounts."

"Anita confronted Frances, who just laughed. All the time she'd been working for Anita, she had her own shops and was just trying to get at Anita's suppliers. Like, who does that, Claudia?"

"Who indeed." Claudia considered for a moment. "Sahana, would your friend see Frances as someone who was led by her husband?"

Sahana laughed. "I can answer that for you. Not a chance! I've seen her myself, berating him. My word! She roared at him, like a sergeant major. He was definitely not the leader in that marriage, in my opinion."

Claudia thanked her and went back to Brigade meeting business. She had some ideas turning over in her head, but they would have to wait until that evening. As soon as she could, she made an excuse to talk to Liza Dunne, an attractive and expensively dressed blonde in her late thirties. Liza harboured dreams of being a recognized socialite and the attention of one of the Brigade's leading ladies made her anxious to please and garrulous.

Oh yes, she was very close to Frances O'Reilly! She gushed and preened a little. In fact, to hear the way Liza told it, she had taken poor dowdy Frances under her wing and helped her find her feet in Dublin. Frances knew nothing about fashion, she hinted, until Liza had given her a few pointers and shown her how to dress. That might have been true, Claudia thought as she considered the woman's outfit. It reminded her of Frances' uniform of expensive but clashing styles, flashy jewellery and even down to the helmet of blonde hair.

"So, they weren't from Dublin?"

Kilkenny was a nice place and all, but hardly comparable to the capital. And that husband of hers, he had good connections - some rich family in the area - but he himself had nothing. Although Frances did like to hint they were in line for an inheritance. She rattled on happily while Claudia nodded and smiled. The smile became a little more fixed as Liza touched on her own affairs, including her husband's irritating ex-wife, not to mention his adult children who were so disapproving of her, his fixation with how his ex-wife afforded a house in the Merrion area and finally, why should Eve have got so much out of the divorce if she could afford Kimberly Cottage?

Claudia let the outpouring of peevish insecurities wash over her head, her hand touching the little stone she carried in her pocket. It was smooth and round with a natural hole in the centre and it was her constant companion. It made dealing with people, and their overpowering energy much easier. As soon as Liza paused for breath, she gently redirected her back to the subject at hand.

"Still, it must have been a shock, the poor man dying like

that. At least Frances has an alibi! You know how people like to gossip, pure waffle of course but still...saying she was very difficult, or they had money problems. I even heard she was definitely seen around the lane, but of course, it can't be true can it? Not if she was in the Merrion Complex all that time!"

Liza paled, underneath her careful makeup. "Eh yes. Of course."

"She was in work, wasn't she?"

To Claudia's surprise, the other woman stuttered a few words of agreement, avoiding eye contact.

"As far as I know," Liza said abruptly. Her entire manner had changed, Claudia noticed. In fact she lost no time in making her excuses to move away quickly, leaving the Brigadier standing alone. Claudia smiled thoughtfully.

At the same time, Granny Goode was carefully reading through comments and private messages left on her YouTube channel. Most were interesting speculations unsupported by any evidence but worth reading in case any of the theories fit the evidence. One or two were more concrete - she learned quite a bit about Eve Caulton's neighbours on Bramble Lane. It was one of the advantages of life in a small city - indeed, a small country. Everyone knew someone, who knew another person, who knew you. Almost all of it was innocuous; Eve Caulton was a better known artist than she had realized and Ronan Desmond was well remembered in his home town of Ennis, in Co. Clare. But there were one or two gems in among them - she took careful notes and sat back to have a comfortable little think for herself.

The afternoon was a busy one, for everyone. Dymphna took her leave of Tom, having invited him to that evening's meeting. She wasn't sure quite how the others would react, but that couldn't be helped. Niamh was waiting for her outside the Merrion Complex, ready for a little undercover snooping. "Frances' car is in the car park, but she isn't in the boutique, I checked."

"Well, let's just wander in anyway and see what happens." They paused outside Frances' shop, eyeing the windows uncertainly. Across the top was a huge sign, with elaborate font spelling out the legend "Chique Chicks" while the clothes themselves, draped on faceless plastic mannequins, were loud and noticeable. Leopard skin tunics fought with neon leggings, and someone had thought fit to pair a purple sequined jacket with a pineapple print dress. The overall effect was eye-catching, to say the least.

"Oh," Niamh said faintly, "It's not what I expected."

"Definitely not our demographic," Dymphna agreed. "I think we need a cover story."

Sure enough, the moment they entered the store, one of the tall, willowy assistants made a beeline for the two women. "Can I help you, ladies?" The girl spoke in a careful imitation of the accent known as a "D4" after the expensive postcode that spawned it. Every vowel was strangled and drawled. Underneath, there were still traces of a more natural, Dublin accent. She looked at the older ladies doubtfully. They looked like her Granny, who wouldn't be seen dead in a place like "Chique Chicks."

"Um, are you looking for anything in particular?" "Oh yes, dear!" Niamh said brightly. "My granddaughter has a birthday coming up, and I'm trying to find a present for her. She mentioned that she loved some jewellery she saw here, a few weeks ago. I thought we'd take a chance....see if we could find a piece."

The girl's face cleared. "Oh, good. Yes." Privately she thanked heavens they weren't hoping to waltz out of there wearing a pink glitter jumpsuit. "We have several lovely sets, handmade by local makers and a range of glamourous costume jewellery that is majorly in, right now. Chloe Una Forbes wore them in her latest Instagram story..."

A bewildering array of accessories were passed in front of their eyes, Niamh choosing the least gaudy of a set featuring crystals and faux pearls. Their sales assistant, Amanda, turned out to be conscientious and considerate, especially once she relaxed and forgot she was supposed to be frosty and exclusive. By the time she was ready to ring up their purchases, they were all on the best of terms. Amanda confided that she was the eldest of three girls, her mother was a single mother and her father hadn't been seen since a particularly raucous week at the Galway Races, circa twenty-thirteen.

"Not that he was missed," she said matter-of-factly. "You can't miss someone who is never there. Poor Mam felt it though. But sure, aren't we all doing well? I have this job, and I bartend at the weekends. Deadly club in town, I love it. Both my sisters are still in school. They are doing brilliantly."

"Your mother must be very proud," Niamh said warmly. "Three great girls, what more could a Mammy want?" "Ah she is, especially of my sisters. Claire's the youngest and she's just a genius at art. Sheila is doing her Leaving Cert this year and she'll be off to college, honest she's dead clever. I was never any use at school, but she's going to go all the way," Pride beamed from Amanda's eyes.

"And I bet you help out with that," Niamh said gently.

"Sure, what else are big sisters for?" Amanda grinned. "I'll never set the world on fire, but that pair! They'll be out winning prizes for all sorts, mark my words."

Niamh and Dymphna exchanged a look and Dymphna fished in her purse for a coin. She pulled out a small, old fashioned coin with a hole in it.

"Give me your hand, dear," she said. Amanda stuck out her hand, and the older woman rubbed it with the coin, then pressed a two euro piece into her hand. "Have you never heard of Hanselling?"

Amanda shook her head, but held on tightly to the coin, smiling.

"It's an old Dublin tradition. Some people have the knack of it. Dymphna here, she has it. Hanselling means you'll never want. Time was when no one would use a new purse or wallet without having it done. It's why you should never give either of those things without putting a few euros in them. And everyone wanted their babies hanselled for good fortune. Someone with the gift of it would press some coins into a baby's hand. It kept poverty at bay."

"Oh! That's so cool, thank you," Amanda held up her hand and stared at it in wonder. "Hey, maybe I'll get a raise." From her tone, the ladies guessed that was as unlikely as a lottery win.

"Boss a bit mean, is he?"

"She, actually. Mrs. O'Reilly. You possibly have heard of her? Her husband died...well, was murdered recently. In one of those cottages off the main road."

"No! Not that stabbing? That's awful. The poor woman, I feel a bit mean now."

"Don't." Amanda snorted. "She's not a nice person."

"Were they close? She and the husband, I mean."

"Hmm. You know what, I think they kind of got on together,

in the way that two horrible people get on. Like, in school, there's two bullies so they team up with each other? But I always feel like she only cares about herself. She's not exactly weeping over him - far more interested in the insurance than in the funeral arrangements."

"I suppose she has an alibi for the murder," Niamh asked.

"She does." Amanda said glumly. "Me."

# Chapter 17

**M**rs. Moriarty and Niamh Caulton were the first to arrive at Kimberly Cottage, both carrying dishes covered in tin foil. Eve sniffed appreciatively. "If this goes on much longer, I'll be the size of a house. What's on the menu tonight?"

"Lamb, in gravy with all the trimmings." Her mother made herself at home, laying the table and fussing around the kitchen. "Dymphna and I made the lamb and Claudia is bringing most of the trimmings."

"You know there's enough lamb there to feed a small army?"

"Ah. Well, there'll be a good few of us," Niamh murmured.

"Four, five, six...there's a lot there for six of us." Eve replied.

"Eight," Dymphna busied herself, avoiding Eve's eye.

"Eight? Who else is coming?"

Her mother and neighbour exchanged one of their looks.

"I invited Tom MacDonagh,"

"Tom? Tom, our chief suspect?"

"Tom, our neighbour who wants to help."

Eve took a deep breath. "That's still only seven."

"Well, I thought it was time we talked to Ronan Desmond."

"Detective Desmond, who is investigating this murder and who thinks I'm his chief suspect?"

"Yes. Don't be in the way, dear. If you must stand around chatting, set the table at least."

Claudia arrived just in time to prevent Eve replying. She was loaded up with dishes and containers, a feast of roast potatoes, parsnips, carrots, petits pois and more, all of which were cooked to perfection. Eve was thoroughly redundant in her own kitchen and resigned herself to making teas and coffees, and greeting the rest of her guests. Jo Maguire was next to arrive, with her grandmother. Greta was resplendent in a shiny tracksuit that had the designer's name displayed everywhere, and a selection of gold jewellery.

"I thought I'd make an effort," she confided in a whisper that could be heard two streets away, "Seeing as there shall be gentlemen present."

Jo rolled her eyes and mouthed, "My boss! They invited my boss."

Poor Jo! Eve ushered her into the living room, while Greta trotted off into the kitchen. "I'm so sorry, Jo, I only found out a few minutes ago."

"She told me on your doorstep," Jo replied bitterly. "She knew fine well I wouldn't have come, and she wanted me to drive. She's two glasses of sherry in her already, heaven only knows what she'll say."

Eve was spared the need to reply as the doorbell went again. Her little house was getting quite crowded already, but the arrival of both Tom and Ronan at the same time made it shrink. Neither were small men, although both seemed to be intent on fading into the background as much as possible. Ronan looked alarmed as four elderly women fluttered around him. Eve felt quite sorry for him, knowing they were playing him like a fiddle. Then the memory of him grilling her for several hours in that smelly interrogation room eased her conscience.

Tom made himself useful, producing an electric screwdriver, and a door security chain. "I can fit this for you," he offered shyly. Eve nodded, quite touched. True to his word, ten minutes work produced a well-fitted chain that she could use to vet callers to the door.

At last dinner was on the table, and the eight of them managed to squeeze around the small dining area. Tom had fetched in two extra seats from the garden furniture, not all the plates and cups matched and there was more than one person elbowed in the ribs by their neighbour. However, the food was delicious, and the banter flowed around the table. Even Detective Desmond cheered up and managed a few pleasantries. By common consent, no one mentioned the murder case, until the table was cleared and everyone had retired to the living room and found a perch. Eve distributed a fresh round of refreshments, including some beer and wine. She settled herself in the last chair and looked around expectantly.

"Who is going first?"

"I am," Tom said, looking sheepish. "I should clear up a few things, I think. Ronan, I never thought any of this was important until Dymphna came to talk to me today but I owe you an apology. I should have thought to tell you, I realize that now."

He repeated his explanation of the row he had with Brian O'Reilly, simply and without embellishment. Eve was conscious of a wave of relief as he put forward his story. It had bothered her to think he might not be the friendly, decent man he seemed to be - although it was obvious Margaret Furey brought out the chivalry in more than Ronan Desmond. And how was Detective Desmond reacting to the story? Ronan's face gave little away, but Eve was sure she spotted an appreciative twitch of the mouth as Tom described wanting to box Brian's ears.

"And you're sure that is everything, Tom? You didn't continue the row later on, or at any other time?" "On my word of honour, I never mentioned it again, neither did he. In fact, we didn't speak after that." "Okay. That's interesting information, thank you." "I'm sure there's nothing in it, though. He was just trying to sound important."

Dymphna shook her head. "It's no use, Tom. We are fairly sure he was blackmailing her, in some way. He and that wife of his found out something about Margaret's past and were using it against her. I'm sorry, Ronan but that's why we invited you here. I know you care about her. We all do. But she is going about this all wrong, hiding away and terrified. She needs to face this head on and deal with it."

"Blackmail?"

"Of a sort. Look, I will tackle her again tomorrow but all you need to know is that Brian got her to help him break in here."

"Forced her to help?" Ronan asked sharply. "Yes. She absolutely didn't want to, and I doubt she had anything to do with what happened to him, but she was in a tight spot. She's afraid that admitting her role in what happened will not only ruin her position as a teacher, it will make her your main suspect."

Ronan's face was a mix of exasperation and pity. "She must be in bits."

"She is. But like I said, leave her to me."

Claudia interrupted. "Never mind Margaret. Anyone like to hear what I found out today?"

She grinned at their faces. "Frances O'Reilly is not only the owner of the boutique here in Merrion, but she also owns three more across the country. One in Kilkenny, and one each in Galway and Cork. I dug into their background and Brian was connected to rich O'Reilly's in Kilkenny - Frances liked to say they were in line for an inheritance. But here's the real scoop. Frances is best friends with Liza Dunne. Eve's...well, her ex-husband's current wife, I suppose." Dead silence greeted this. Eve felt her cheeks blush, a hot wave that started at her neck. Niamh gave an explosive snort that managed to combine shock and contempt. Everyone else looked sympathetic.

"It's fine," Eve managed. "Look, we've both moved on. Please, Claudia, tell us what she said." "That's the way," Tom MacDonagh raised his glass to her. "Onwards and Upwards!"

"Sorry, Eve, but I never connected her to you til this afternoon. But of course, your ex-husband has been pumping your kids for information ever since you bought the cottage, and Liza is feeling a bit insecure. She confided in Frances. Your ex can't understand how you managed it, thinks you either got a huge mortgage or have hidden income. He's eaten up with jealousy and suspicion, was the impression she gave me. Liza met up with Frances socially the night before the murder and it sounds like she gave her chapter and verse on you."

Wow. Eve needed to sit somewhere alone and turn over this information in her mind. Peter, jealous that she managed to move on while he had already wed his girlfriend the moment Irish law allowed - what a thoroughly unpleasant man he was, really.

"But does that have any bearing on the murder?"

"I'm not sure, except that Frances knew a lot more about you than any of us suspected. What might have more relevance is this "inheritance" they hinted at. Liza said she pressed Frances once, expecting her to say it was an elderly relative or something. Instead she became very coy and talked about how it was Brian's by right but some people would seize on it if they could."

"I might be able to explain..." Both Eve and Jo spoke in unison.

"You go first," Jo grinned. "It's your house after all."

"If you're sure? Then, as you know - well, most of you know - I was following up on the diary.."

"Diary?" Ronan Desmond groaned. "What's this about a diary?"

"Oh." Eve recounted finding the journal and the contents. The detective looked around at them grimly, his eye lighting on Jo Maguire for a shade too long. "If, and I say If, there was some kind of investigation going on behind my back, and evidence was being withheld..."

"Don't be daft," Granny Goode snapped her fingers at him. "What could an old journal possibly have to do with a murder? How could anyone guess they'd be connected? We were researching the history of the cottage, and fell across some interesting information by accident. Which we are now giving to you. What's the problem with that, I'd like to know?"

She glowered up at him. Ronan knew when to beat a tactical retreat.

"Grand so. If that's your story. I beg your pardon, Ms. Caulton, please continue. You contacted the Farrells..."

"Eve. And yes, I talked to Seamus Farrell. He's a lovely man, with a huge interest in his family's history. And he was close to Julia before she died. He sent me the manuscript he's written, all the stories she told him. I can give you all a copy but to save time, I thought I would just recount the bits that affect us?" Everyone nodded.

"Okay. Well, the last we knew of her Julia was trapped. Her

mother and Uncle William were determined to send her off to be a poor relative in her cousin's household in England. Julia was confined to the house and Con was barred. Uncle William said he would have the union annulled - but it sounded as if he was set on sending her away regardless of the status of the marriage."

"But it seems he reckoned without the residents of Bramble Lane. They were generally working-class, poor, some uneducated and others reasonably educated for the day. Julia relied on a girl called Kathleen, whose mother sent her to the O'Reillys to teach Julia how to keep house. Having lost her father and without an income, Julia had to learn all these things from scratch. In Seamus' story, Julia gave their full names - Kathleen and her mother Nellie Kelly. Kathleen called to the house as usual, only to be turned away by Mrs. O'Reilly, boasting about how she would soon have a new maid. A bit hurt, Kathleen was inclined to let it go but she ran into Con Farrell. He was distraught, worrying about Julia and ready to storm the house after a few days. Kathleen persuaded him to calm down and let her try again. The Farrells and the Kellys had a conference, which ended in Mrs. Kelly and Kathleen calling to Kimberly Cottage. Mrs. Kelly went to the front door, and berated Mrs. O'Reilly loudly and at length for being rude to "*her Kathleen, what had done them such favours!*" In the meantime, Kathleen Kelly - with the aid of Con Farrell - got over the back wall. She then threw pebbles at the back windows until Julia appeared and opened one. Kathleen got the story from her, under cover of the noise her mother was making at the front door. She told Julia to hold tight, that they would make a plan and she would get word to her. The enterprising Kathleen clambered back over into her own garden, according to Julia the kid was "*not hampered by her long skirts, but hitched them up like a washerwoman, her bloomers showing*! She comes across as a formidable young woman."

"Now, a lot of the stories Julia told Seamus weren't in neat, chronological order. He's had to make a few guesses here and there. He says there were several hiding places in the house, made by Con but the idea to make them came from the fact that Julia saw her mother hiding something in a hole in the bookcase. Her mother never knew she saw, but it made a deep impression on the young Julia. Mrs. O'Reilly had kept back some jewelry, including a very expensive jewel on a pendant, and a few other personal items from the bailiffs when their father's debts had come to light. Julia didn't begrudge her, she felt it was too hard on her mother to ask her to sell them even when they were penniless. In later life, she wondered if her Uncle's supposed kindness to them was based on his desire to get the jewels from her mother at some point, even after death. Maybe her mother was canny enough to know this and used it to get William onside - after all, you'd think he'd be happy to see his indigent relative married to a doctor and off his hands."

"A jewel." Eve's audience was enthralled.

"Yes. So you see, if we assume that there was a jewel, and Mrs. O'Reilly succeeded in keeping it away from William til the bitter end, maybe that's what Brian was looking for."

Ronan Desmond nodded slowly. "It sounds fantastic but yes, a valuable jewel might be worth a spot of trespassing to O'Reilly."

"But what happened to Julia?" Tom MacDonagh leaned forward. His eyes were bright with interest.

"Ah yes! Kathleen returned later that day, with a bundle of tools in a pouch. Julia let down a makeshift rope and the tools were hoisted up to her bedroom. Con's work tools, and instructions on how to jimmy open the lock on her bedroom door. The plan was set for that night. In her own words... "*It was near midnight before my mother's snores convinced me to try. It took some force to break that lock, and I was shaking with fear at every single noise it made. I was sure she would hear and come investigate, but not a stir from her! At last the latch gave way and the door was unlocked and I could sneak out. I crept down the stairs, clutching my clothes and the picture of my father that stood by my bed. I didn't even dare retrieve my journal from its hiding place, every second was of such importance. I knew there was no point in trying the front door, Mother had it triple locked and the key in bed with her. But the back door was not so heavily sealed, and I knew the trick of jiggling the key until it gave way, so after a few false starts it too opened. I stepped out into the garden, my first free breath in days filling my lungs. I had only gone two steps before I saw two figures waiting for me, Con and his father. They lifted two sections of the high fence away and I stepped through it into the neighbouring garden. The boards were replaced behind me and that was it. Julia O'Reilly was gone and in her place – Mrs. Julia Farrell.*""*

A round of applause greeted this, and a cheer from Granny Goode. "It's still a bit sad though," Eve reminded them. "She never spoke to her mother again, and she never forgave her. When the mother died she left everything to Julia, or her offspring if she predeceased her, but Julia never came to collect. At some point prior, and we don't know how, Mrs. O'Reilly bought Kimberly from William. Same story, she left it to her daughter but Julia couldn't bear to return here so she sold it on. But on the plus side, she had a great marriage. Con built up a thriving practice, their daughter runs it now, Seamus went into computers and he and his family live in the house Con and

Julia eventually bought. They are a happy, united bunch and obviously loved their grandparents."

"I'm so glad," Niamh dabbed at her eyes.

"Let me write this out," Tom had a small notebook and pen and was scribbling furiously. "So far, you've discovered a lot of information, but we need to see where it intersects."

"Well, while you're doing that, want to hear my story?" Jo Maguire grinned.

All heads turned in her direction; satisfied with the response she sat back and continued, "I searched this house from top to bottom. The full works, no nook left unexamined." She risked a look in Ronan's direction. "In my spare time, obviously, and solely to further the "historical research." I found two other hiding places, both in the bookcase. They had some bits and pieces in them. Old coins, this old savings book and two large silver frames. Tom, you'd be the man to value them. Might be worth a few bob. But then I found one, set into the wall beside the fireplace, behind a brick. Very small, just big enough to get a hand in. And this was in it."

She stuck out one hand, to show a battered jeweller's box. It clicked open when she applied pressure to a small metal clasp at the front, the lid of the box snapping up to reveal...

"It's empty!'

# Chapter 18

"Oh!" Eve couldn't hide her disappointment. "I thought you'd found something there for a moment."

"But I did," Jo said happily. "You're thinking like an artist, or a romance novelist. I'm thinking like a cop."

Ronan stared at her and then smiled slowly. "I think I follow you, Jo."

"I should hope you do, and you the highly paid detective...*sir*." She looked like a cheeky but happy schoolgirl. "Look, if we found the jewel, we would have a nice story to tell Julia's family. But without the jewel, we have a shot at finding our murder."

"But how?"

"Because we have a reasonable idea that the jewellery was never found, not until the day Brian was killed. He was looking for the pendant jewel, I'll bet my last chocolate biscuit on it. And if he got in here to find it..."

"Oh!" Greta sat bolt upright. "If he found it, and the killer took it...if the killer murdered him for it..."

"Then when we find the jewel, we find our killer." Jo finished triumphantly.

"It's not that simple," Ronan said. Everyone looked at him expectantly. "Don't get me wrong, it's a theory. It hangs together. But there's no proof that he knew about the jewel.

There's no way of proving the jewel was even there. If it was a jewel."

"It was a jewel," Eve said, "Or more precisely a necklace with a jewel. It's in the story Seamus Farrell sent. Julia saw her mother hiding stuff that she had managed to rescue from the Bailiffs."

"Okay," Ronan conceded. "It's likely. But how can you be sure it was there when Brian was murdered?"

Jo chewed her lip. "I can't be one hundred percent sure."

"We still have one line of attack," Dymphna said. "I'm sure Margaret knows why he was here and more, I'm sure she had a hand in it. Oh, don't bridle up on me, Ronan Desmond. I'm not saying she killed him. But she knows more than she's letting on. I'm going to tackle her first thing in the morning."

Ronan looked like he would like to object but he said nothing.

"It's the best plan," Eve said soothingly. "If you interrogate her, Ronan, she'll just withdraw again. Even if she tells you something, you have to go through official channels. Let Dymphna have another go, and if we can get the story out of her unofficially, we might be able to help her. "

He flushed, a dull red on both cheeks. "I have to do my job."

"Of course you do, and that's why it's best left to us." Dymphna said smugly. "We'll let you know anything you need to know."

Ronan's face was a picture of warring emotions. The police-man in him wanted to protest but the young man who liked his neighbour Margaret very much indeed, thought this would be a way out of a horrible situation. After all, he reasoned, no man wants to arrest the girl he fancies and especially not for murder. Dymphna was an elder lady, concerned about a young woman. He couldn't stop her from calling and asking how she was...

"Okay. But go easy, and you tell me anything you find out."

"I'll go easy," promised Dymphna. Eve noticed she didn't promise the rest.

"Great work, Jo," Niamh said. "And we had an interesting chat too, didn't we Dymphna?"

"Ah yes, young Amanda."

"Amanda is Frances' sales assistant in her shop. We popped in, which reminds me I bought a necklace and earring set that I'll have to give someone. Don't let me forget, Eve. Where was I? Yes, the boutique. Awful place, I can't imagine who wears that stuff. Your Peter's new girlie, I suppose. And maybe I'm just old and out of touch, and God knows I think girls should wear whatever they please. But it's terrible really, you'd hate it." Eve wasn't sure if her mother meant everyone or just her. "Anyway, lovely young girl in there. She's got a mother and sisters to support, and she hates Frances. I'd say she would love to be able to say she wasn't there, that afternoon. But she was, and there you have it."

A moment's silence ensued as everyone tried to untangle Niamh's report.

"You're saying this Amanda is sure Frances didn't leave?"

"Sadly yes." Niamh didn't look sad about it, she looked smug.

"But - but that ruins everything." Jo's dismay was comical. "She was our prime suspect."

"She still is," Niamh replied. "Listen, now. Frances was definitely there in the morning. She made herself thoroughly unpleasant, and Amanda was run ragged by her. Then after twelve o'clock, there was a sudden change of heart. Frances started sucking up to her, asking her would she like to take an early lunch? Told her to take a nice long lunch too, that she would man the shop. Well, Amanda does go for lunch,

143

and knowing what her employer is like, she took the hour - no more or less. She felt sure that if she took more, Frances would change gears, say she was late and deny having given her permission. When she got back, Amanda said Frances *was* there, serving a customer. But she looked frazzled, a bit hot and bothered and dusty. And there were some small green leafs in her hair and caught on her jacket."

"But all this is way before Brian was murdered," Eve pointed out. "I was still here eating lunch at one o'clock."

"Ah will ya listen? I know that. But she was definitely up to something that morning. I think with a bit of digging we can break this alibi." Niamh smiled complacently. "If we only had access to CCTV footage, or knew a Garda who did..."

Ronan stared at her. "Do you think we're a shower of eejits? I checked every camera from the Merrion to here. There's no..."

"For what time?" Niamh replied. "What time? Well, for... "He paused. "Okay for between two and three in the afternoon, because that's when the murder occurred."

"Check again," Niamh advised. "Check between twelve and one and if you don't see Frances O'Reilly legging it across the road and down into Bramble Lane, on foot, I'll eat my hat."

Ronan nodded slowly. "Okay, that's interesting. I can't see how it changes the fact that this Amanda saw Frances O'Reilly, in work, at the time of the murder."

Claudia raised her hand. "I wonder...tell me exactly what Frances' alibi looks like. The details I mean, not just "she was in work."

"When we say, "at work," to be scrupulous about it, she was at lunch but in full view of Amanda, and several others. The Merrion is busy during office lunch hours, twelve to one, but it's much quieter in the afternoon on a weekday. There's a coffee shop directly across from the boutique, Frances took her lunch there at two pm sharp, sat in a window seat and is clearly seen on CCTV cameras and by people shopping. And of course, her employees who kept an eye on her for their own reasons. Everyone agrees, she went to the bathroom at about ten to three, by which time her husband was dead. She was only in the loo for about ten minutes, anyway. Nowhere near enough time to get over here and back."

Claudia stared into space, her minding whirring. If she saw each piece as a fragment of the whole, and just let them spin and move until they fitted...she could walk back through the days since then, let the hours spin back...and now she was standing in the shopping centre, the boutique on one side and the coffee shop on the other. Frances sitting in the window, Frances hurrying to the toilet...

"Which toilet?"

"Sorry?" "There's a loo in the coffee shop for customers only and then a large bathroom facility upstairs for the whole centre. Where did she go to?"

"The main one, the large public one."

"Why? When there was one right there, handy?"

Ronan shrugged. "It was engaged, maybe? She preferred the ones upstairs? I don't know."

"I think I know. No, no - I'm not sure. It's only the germ of an idea but leave it with me."

Eve felt a bit deflated. "It's getting more complicated, not less."

"That's the way of it, with any investigation," Jo said confidently. "It's all the new information, but we still have no solutions. We're much further on than you think. We have a good idea why Brian was here, Claudia might be able to break the widow's alibi, and Dymphna will bend Margaret to her iron will and force her to confess, won't you Mrs. Moriarty?"

"You're a cheeky whelp," Dymphna said. "If I wasn't so fond of you, I'd bend you to my will and see how you like it."

"Stop squabbling," Greta said. "If no one else has anything to add? Right then, it's my turn. I've had a huge response to my video, people are mad interested in the case. A lot of it is pure nonsense, of course. Some people could make a conspiracy theory out of anything. But there's some interesting bits and pieces and one in particular you'll enjoy." She shuffled a sheaf of papers, printouts of comments and messages collated over the afternoon. "Most of these are about all of ye. I'll start with you, Eve - people like your work a lot. I must say, I didn't realize you were famous."

"I'm not," Eve protested. "I'd be "moderately well known," at the outside."

"Whatever you say. You're well enough known for my audience to have heard of you, and they like your work. Ronan, the GAA club in your hometown think highly of you. Not a one of them doubt you'll solve this murder in record time. Tom, at least three ladies gave you a character reference, they won't hear a word against a fine, good-looking man like yourself. Parents of kids in St. Malachy's are full sure Margaret is innocent and think it's a disgrace the way the fascist forces of law and order are oppressing her," Greta grinned at Ronan, who looked a very unlikely lackey of fascism with his worried face and air of quiet kindness. "But the O'Reilly's...loathed by all who met them. Even family."

"You heard from their family?"

"Yes! From Brian O'Reilly's rich cousins, no less." She grimaced. "Brian was a thorn in their sides, no doubt about it. I spoke personally to two of them, in the end. Anna and her brother Phil. Here's their contact details, Ronan, before I forget. Both agree that Brian was, and I quote, "*A nasty little toad, and no loss.*" Obsessed with money, constantly snooping around and I am sure none of us will be shocked to hear, had attempted a little light blackmail on his more affluent relations. Just low key things, finding out a wee secret they would prefer not to have spread around the area and letting them know he knew. Then a separate request to invest or lend money to one of his ventures. Funny thing is, he was well off himself in the end. Mainly through Frances' businesses, rather than anything he did. But still, he didn't need to put pressure on people like that."

"Which suggests he enjoyed it," Ronan said.

"Exactly. Not a nice man. Frances seems to have been a bit less offensive. Anna said she used to get on quite well with her when they first met her. Phil too, he said she made herself pleasant at first. However, a few years ago, about 2015, there was an incident in Anna's house at a family gathering. Anna's husband caught Francis going through a filing cabinet in his office!"

Tom whistled. "Any idea what she was looking for?"

"No, they couldn't imagine. But Phil said Brian was always making comments about how "lucky" they were to have inherited money. His father did inherit family money but squandered it. Brian didn't see it that way, though. He thought he had somehow been cheated out of a share, by the rest of the family. Anna thinks Francis was looking for some family papers, it could even have been the bill of sale of Kimberly Cottage. That's just my own guess, mind you."

"This is good information," Ronan said. Greta smiled complacently. "It certainly supports the idea that the O'Reilly's were interested in the Cottage."

"They also confirmed something else. It didn't mean much to me until Jo showed us what she had discovered. Anna O'Reilly says Brian was obsessed with stories in their side of the family about the other O'Reilly's. Their Grandfather or great granddad, I lost track, William was very bitter about the Julia O'Reilly branch and often spoke ill of the mother. Said the old woman had stiffed him on a deal, had promised him something and reneged. I bet it was whatever jewelry she had hidden away from the Bailiffs."

This produced another quarter of an hour of excited speculation, but eventually it petered out.

Eve stifled a yawn. "I'm sorry, everyone. I'm absolutely exhausted. There's a lot to sift through here but it'll have to wait until morning. If I don't get to bed soon, I'll fall asleep face first into a water-colour in the morning."

"It's late," Dymphna agreed. "I think we all need to sleep on this. Great work all round though. Tom, thanks for coming. I hope you're agreed, we need to help Margaret come clean about whatever Brian had over her?"

"Yes, I'm in full agreement. We could tackle her together, tomorrow?"

Dymphna nodded. "Grand, so. Maybe we can reconvene afterwards, anyone who is free?"

Ronan was clearly turning a deaf ear to the talk of investigating, but he flashed a grateful look at the older lady as he gathered his jacket and notebook. Eve hid a smile; the young detective was very transparent in his regard for the teacher, no matter what trouble she was in.

"We'll help her," she said reassuringly, "I bet it's something relatively small, once we get to the bottom of it."

Claudia wanted to visit Chique Chicks and meet Amanda for herself. She was sure if she could just see the scene, something might click. Niamh said she would team up with Tom, go over everything they had learned so far. Jo had work but assured them her brilliant mind would be busy mulling over everything.

"Sure, I'll have it cracked by lunchtime," She grinned at her boss' back and wiggled her eyebrows. Eve was sure Ronan knew but was wisely ignoring the irrepressible Jo. Greta offered her services to anyone who needed them, unless new information was volunteered by one of her listeners. "But we're getting close, I feel it."

Once her guests had left, Eve threw the last few dishes in the dishwasher and retired to bed. It was another clear, mild night and she opened a window for air. Nothing like some cool night air, she thought. Peter had hated sleeping with windows open but now she could please herself. How odd a coincidence, that Liza Dunne was friends with Frances O'Reilly. But Dublin was a small city compared to most European capitals. And social climbing ladies of a certain age was a small demographic. Probably not that wild a chance when you thought about it. Her last, sleepy thought was that Tom had been very sweet, when Peter's name came up. Onwards and upwards, that was a good motto...

Shortly after midnight a small black creature fluttered against the open window. It perched briefly on her windowsill, and peered inside the room. If Eve had been awake, she might have caught a high pitched squeak that sounded suspiciously like a swear word, followed by a muttered, "Wrong house, again." The bat turned itself around, gave a slightly uncertain wobble before gliding away and landing in the next door garden.

A muffled "Ow!" was followed by the sound of Dymphna Moriarty banging her back door shut firmly. "I'm getting too old for this," Dymphna thought. But it was the easiest way to hang out in Margaret's garden and keep an eye on her. She couldn't settle until she knew the girl had bolted her doors and turned her alarm on. It was quite clear to her that the young teacher could be described as a "loose end," especially until she finally opened up about her role in things. And anyone ruthless enough to commit murder in a neighbour's living room wouldn't hesitate to tie up loose ends.

Long after her neighbours were asleep in bed, Dymphna lay awake and worried.

# Chapter 19

Eve was awake bright and early, answering emails. There were two from people requesting prices on some pieces she had listed on her website. Both had the price clearly marked online but people always thought there was room to negotiate. Eve was used to it, although as an artist it would be nice for once if someone just paid the asking price without haggling. She replied as firmly and politely as she could, then moved on. In her experience a serious buyer would come back quickly and pay the correct price while time wasters would tie you up for hours in pointless back and forth, then not buy in the end anyway. All part of an artist's life, she reminded herself. It was easier than ever to sell directly without relying on a gallery or agent, but it meant being your own marketer, agent and business director.

There was one last email, from a Lesley Dylan, requesting prices for a commission. The brief was very vague, referencing a series Eve had done a few years before, landscapes painted in a dreamy, hazy style full of colour and peace. It had been very well received and even reported on in the Arts section of a popular newspaper. This Lesley person wanted something *"Similar but in a different palate and maybe not a landscape,"* which was infuriating but also not terribly unusual. Rolling her eyes, Eve fired off a generic response outlining the average cost of commission pieces and requesting clearer information.

Feeling very virtuous at doing so much work before eleven a.m. she eyed her corner studio longingly. It would be a good day to get stuck in, it had been days since she had painted. Within minutes she was deep in an imaginary painting, based on the autumnal colours in the gardens of Bramble lane.

The doorbell shattered her daydream, a persistent buzzing. Someone had their finger on the bell and was determined to be heard. Eve approached the door uneasily. The chain that Tom had fitted was still in place since the previous evening. Eve left it there and opened the door a crack. To her surprise, Frances O'Reilly was on the doorstep. The woman looked angrily at the door, obviously unaware that Eve could see her because once it dawned on her, she hastily rearranged her face into a smile.

"Hi! Eve? Open the door, for goodness' sake. It's chilly out here."

Eve closed the door, removed the chain, and reopened it.

"Mrs. O'Reilly –Frances. You startled me. Can I help you?"

Considering how much Frances had been on her mind over the preceding days, it was a shock to remember that strictly speaking they had never formally been introduced. While having one's husband murdered in a neighbour's living room was a sort of connection, she supposed, it did not leave much room for the social conventions. "Is everything okay?"

"Yes. Well, as well as can be expected. Obviously." Frances looked at her expectantly and gave an exaggerated shiver by way of a hint. Eve had been reared with very strict principles when it came to hospitality, but she steeled herself. Asking Frances in, when they were reasonably sure she had killed her husband struck her as a social minefield. Stepping out onto the doorstep, Eve pulled the door over behind her, blocking the neighbour's view of her hallway.

"I'm glad you're doing okay. Was there something I could help you with?"

"Can't we step inside?" Frances complained. "It's very chilly." She was wearing a green blouse with poppies patterned across it, very eye catching if slightly too bright for Eve's artistic taste. It was certainly too thin for an Autumn day in Ireland, no matter how mild.

"I'm so sorry, I'm afraid not. I'm in the middle of work, you see. Paint everywhere, sketches. You understand, I'm sure. So, can I help you?"

"I was hoping to talk to you, about the...about the circum-stances of my husband's death."

"Oh. I'm so sorry for your loss, obviously, but I don't know what happened. I wandered in after the fact, you see. I'm sure the Gardaí have told you?"

"Well, yes. Of course. But it happened in your house." Frances replied with some asperity. "Your living room. And I'm sure you can understand how difficult this all is for me."

"As I said, I'm so sorry. It must be traumatic for you." Eve nodded sympathetically but refused to budge. "It did happen in my home, yes, but that's something I'd like to forget. It won't do any good to dwell on it, will it? I'm trying to get back to normal, to be honest."

"Well for you!" the widow shot back, bitterly. "I can't get back to normal, not with his killer wandering around the place, free as a bird."

Eve didn't know what to respond to this. She just tried to look concerned. Frances eyed her, waiting for a response but gave up once it was clear that Eve wasn't going to be drawn. "Margaret

Furey, for goodness sake woman! She's obviously the killer, standing over his body like that. From what the detectives say, you caught her red-handed. I must say, I expected better of you. Doesn't it bother you that my husband's murderer is out, living practically next door to you? What if it was you she was after all along? We should discuss complaining to the local Superintendent. I don't know about you but I certainly can't feel safe, waiting for her to strike again."

"Strike...Ah here, Frances. I'm awfully sorry about your husband but there isn't a shred of evidence to suggest Margaret was anything other than an innocent bystander."

"An innocent what? Sure, wasn't she in your house. What was she doing there, if not to kill my poor Brian?"

"Well, for that matter - what was Brian doing in my living room in the first place? That's the first question I'd like answered."

Frances stuttered a little, obviously caught off guard. "I-I don't know about that. But I'm sure he was just checking on you. He saw the door open, and found Margaret in your house more than likely. How can anyone be sure she wasn't the first in?"

It was an uncomfortable truth, Eve thought. People who knew the teacher were convinced she was telling the truth about that, but no one knew for sure. She tried not to show her discomfort to Frances, but the truth was, of everyone on Bramble Lane, Margaret was the one with opportunity, and possibly a motive if he was blackmailing her. Maybe they wanted it to be the unpleasant Frances so badly, they were all willfully overlooking the obvious explanation.

But the older ladies, the "old bats" as she had affectionately come to think of them. were convinced she was innocent. And those women had a lifetime of experience, and shrewdness, behind them. Not to mention, their unique, special abilities. Eve stiffened her backbone and faced Frances squarely. "I can't imagine that young woman doing anything so violent."

"Oh, can't you? Fine then! I came here expecting that you'd be a reasonable person. If you're happy to live cheek by jowl with a maniac, that's up to you. Don't come crying to me when she's found standing over another dead body."

"I am sorry, Frances. I do see how this must be upsetting for you, but there's no point harassing the girl. She's terribly upset too and has hardly stirred out since that afternoon. Let's leave everything to the Gardaí, yes?"

Her neighbour strode off without so much as a grunt in reply. Eve retreated back into Kimberly Cottage and looked at her easel sadly. The inspiration had left her, it was hard to think of beauty and nature while this dark question mark hung over everything. Frances was right about one thing, it was horrible to think a killer was living on Bramble Lane and even worse to think that maybe they were chasing the wrong lead. What did any of them know about being detectives anyway? Apart from Ronan Desmond, obviously. He wasn't convinced Margaret was innocent, she thought suddenly. That's why he's so worried.

She turned back to the computer. If the muse was going to desert her, she might as well get some more admin work done. Opening her website, she decided to tackle some of the little clean up jobs she had been putting off, updating her biography and listing some new galleries where her work was on sale. Again, just as she found her groove and was getting something done, the doorbell rang. Swearing under her breath, she opened the door prepared for round two with Frances O'Reilly. Instead there stood Tom, a wooden box filled to the brim with seasonal

155

fruit and vegetables and a sheepish look on his face.

"Hello!" He stuck the box out like an offering. "I wondered if you would like some produce from my garden?"

"Oh. Yes, thank you. They look delicious. Tomatoes, onions, parsnips and what's this at the bottom? Apples! Are they all homegrown?"

"Oh yes. Now the apples are more crab apples, but beautifully tart. It's been an excellent year for my tomatoes, and the rest of my veg are quite decent this year too." He beamed proudly. "I noticed you like to cook, so I hoped these might be useful."

"There's nothing better than homegrown veg," Eve said sincerely. "And the fruit too, I love it. Blackberries and raspberries, what a treat."

"The berries are almost overripe, " Tom warned. "I'd eat them with ice cream tonight, or at least that's what I do. I don't bake much, you see. So it's a dollop of vanilla ice cream, or raspberry ripple and maybe a digestive biscuit broken up into the bowl."

"You've convinced me!" Eve held the door open. "Put them down in the kitchen and I'll get two bowls. I've ice cream in the freezer and even a pack of biscuits around here somewhere. Let's be decadent and have a disgracefully unhealthy lunch."

Tom's eyes lit up. He looked like a mischievous schoolboy as he carried the box of fruit and vegetables into the kitchen. Eve pointed at one of her two armchairs in the living room and instructed him to sit down. Within minutes she brought out a bowl of fruit, ice cream and crushed biscuits. "Here we are!" They tucked in, Tom finishing his slightly ahead of her and grinning contentedly.

"Well, if I'd known you were a woman after my own heart, I'd have been around days ago. I can't remember the last time

I had a treat like that in the middle of the day. I've got awfully stuck in my ways."

"Tell me about it! I'm as bad. It's no fun cooking for one, so I tend to eat the same things over and over. If it wasn't for Dymphna and the ladies feeding me, I wouldn't see a roast potato for months."

"It's the age too," Tom patted his stomach ruefully. "Middle age spread – not that you have any! But I only have to look at one of Dymphna's roast dinners to put on weight."

"Sure, you're fine." And he was, Eve thought. Trim but not skinny. A man who took care of himself for his age but wasn't vain about it. Peter had had an entire bathroom cabinet devoted to his anti aging creams and hair treatments. Tom looked like he just enjoyed life and smiled a lot.

"Do you miss your work, being retired?" The question popped out before it occurred to her it might sound rude. She added hastily, "If you don't mind me asking?"

"Not at all. I loved work, antiques are still my passion. I loved my auction house too, so many nice customers and such interesting pieces. It could be sad too, of course. Someone dies, and we get called in to look at all the things they collected, family pieces, items they bought or received as presents, that no one in the family wants. Or their family needs to sell. We always tried to get a good price for them, though. And I loved going around auctions or poking about in junk sales, the rush when you found something overlooked and discarded that was really a gem in the rough!" He smiled fondly. "Ah, it was a good business. But recently, I realized I was getting older and there were so many things I'd put off. I was married, you know? A wonderful woman, Carol was. She died fifteen years ago and I – I suppose I just worked and worked to cope with that. Suddenly

I was at home alone, no one to share things with - it changed my perspective. My nephew has been my junior partner for years, so I decided, why not let him run the show? While he's still young and full of ideas. And I retired, to grow veg and - well, try to live a little, before it's too late."

Eve grinned. "I know what you mean. Divorce, in my case but for the last few years I've put my life on hold. Even with the new regulations, and with us largely agreeing on finances, it took three and bit years to get the divorce done. Lucky for me, the house sold quickly after that or I would still be living in my mother's house. My art and my lecturing, that's been my life for the last few years. And my kids of course, but they're grown ups now. Out living their lives. That's why I was so happy to move here, it felt like a new start!"

"Did I disturb your work?" He pointed at her prepped easel. "I'm sorry, I should have checked before barging in on you! I forget not everyone is retired and at a loose end, like me."

"It's grand," Eve said. "I had hoped to get stuck in, but I had a visitor. It sort of put me off. Ruined the mood."

"Ah. You have an artist's temperament - sensitive to mood."

"Not overly so, but I suppose every artist is a bit like that."

"Well, I'll get out of your hair, and maybe inspiration will strike again."

Eve laughed. "This was a very enjoyable interruption, so don't apologize. Thanks so much for the fresh food, I prefer it to supermarket produce any day. I envy you the ability to grow food like that - I've always wanted to try. I thought about making raised beds in the back garden, make it easier on my back."

"Let me know when you're doing that, I would love to help. And any excess veg I have, I'll pass your way." Only after Tom left did she realize she had never told him who had called to the door earlier. Unless of course, he had seen the exchange on the doorstep and the garden produce was an excuse to call over? Eve shook herself. "I'm becoming nasty and suspicious," She thought. "Tom is such a nice man, what a way to think about his generosity!" Still, there it was. That little voice that reminded her she knew very little about her neighbours.

She went to pick up the two empty bowls but glanced at her canvas and paused. It was a scene, of course. The remnants of berries and ice cream still visible on the inside of the pastel-coloured crockery. The two spoons at a jaunty angle, the whole sense of a treat enjoyed with gusto. The sunlight hit the table at just the right angle, golden and warm...without thinking she began to sketch, a little smile on her lips.

# Chapter 20

Tom went straight from Eve's to Wisteria Cottage. Dymphna was waiting for him, her dark eyes twinkling. "Nice lunch?" she asked. Tom tried to sound casual. "Yes, very nice, thanks." He wondered how the old woman could possibly know, but long acquaintance with her had taught him not to ask questions. "So how do we play this?"

"Straightforward," came the stern reply. "She's had a few days of quiet and solitude to think things over. I would say she's ready to talk. I plan to ask her a few questions, you look at her in a kindly manner, I give it ten minutes." She produced a large plastic water bottle, filled with lemonade. "Just in case, I've brought some of Claudia's special mixture." Tom opened his mouth to ask but shut it firmly. He had his suspicions about the elders of the community and their "special" potions and libations, but he was of the opinion that there were many things he didn't understand and many things that weren't meant to be understood by mere men.

He stood behind Dymphna as she rang the doorbell to Wisteria Cottage. The bell was shrill, and he winced, imagining poor Margaret getting a fright in her already nervous state. He glanced at the stern, upright back of his neighbour and hoped fervently they were doing the right thing. Ronan Desmond hadn't objected, he comforted himself, and as a detective if he thought it was the wrong move, surely he would have said something!

The door opened a crack, then wider as the young woman recognized her visitors. She was pale, but otherwise composed. *Resigned*, Tom thought, *she looks like she's given up.*

Dymphna didn't wait but stepped into the hall. "We've come for a chat."

"Oh. I'm not feeling so good, Mrs. Moriarty. I'm sorry but –"

"You'll be fine," Dymphna responded. Her tone was bracing, not unkind but not inviting of argument either. "Tom, put the kettle on. Margaret and I are going to have a nice talk."

Margaret tried to object but with an apologetic smile, Tom retreated to the kitchen and started a round of tea. The two women could hear him banging around in search of cups and teabags while the electric kettle boiled.

"Well? Don't leave us here staring at each other, dear."

"I-Oh, come in then!" Margaret didn't sound particularly inviting but Dymphna ignored the reluctance in her voice. "Good girl. Settle yourself down there and listen to me. When I say "chat" I mean an end to this nonsense. You're making yourself ill, shut away in here. Whatever trouble has brought you to this, you're not making it any better. You look guilty, not to put a tooth in it. Oh, I know, I know, no need to interrupt me. It's none of my business, you just want to be left alone...I get it and you're wrong." "You have friends, Margaret. People who care about you. Neighbours, and one young man who is risking his career because he can't bring himself to think of you as guilty. It's not just your business, is it? Incidentally, none of us think you're a killer."

Margaret sat back, her face changing colour rapidly from pale to red to a more normal, healthy hue. She closed her eyes but still didn't speak.

"We can't help you," Dymphna continued quietly, "unless we know what is wrong. Let me tell you what we know so far. We know there's something in your past, from when you were young, that Brian O'Reilly found out about and held over your head. Whatever it was, it was bad enough to put you in his power. Using this secret, he persuaded you to steal the key to Kimberly Cottage - I suspect while he was away on holiday? You were to give it to him when he returned, but he came home to find Eve already living there. A normal person would have had the sense to wait a while but Brian was impatient. As soon Eve went out and the place was empty, he let himself in."

Tom could feel the tension from the other room. He held his breath, for what seemed ages, until at last he heard the younger woman's voice reply. She spoke quietly, sadly.

"He was so insistent. I thought in the end, what harm? It had been lying empty since poor Mrs. Williams went into Willowbrook. I did have a set of keys to the front door. I'd run some errands months ago for Mrs. Williams and she gave me a set she rarely used. An emergency spare, she called it. I meant to return them, but I just forgot. I mentioned it once to Brian, in passing, saying I had to remember to replace them. It was after she'd gone to the nursing home, you see, and it slipped my mind. When he demanded the set, I said no at first but when he threatened me-I was afraid of what he would do, and I figured it wasn't like there was much to steal. He'll let himself in, have a poke around and leave. Then Ms. Caulton moved in - I told him he couldn't possibly risk going in but he insisted on taking the key anyway. Said he had talked to her and she was as stubborn as Maud Williams. I *begged* him not to use the key, but he wouldn't listen. He was unstable. It had become some kind of obsession, to get inside Kimberly. I thought he would at least wait a while, maybe until the owner went away for a weekend or something. But on Wednesday, I was coming home from St. Malachy's and saw Ms. Caulton as she left for a walk, and then spotted Brian letting himself in. He must have been mad - it was obvious she was only out for a stroll, she turned to walk down the lane not towards the main road. I couldn't bear it, I knew if he got caught red-handed, he would say I gave him the key. If he was going to be in trouble, he'd make sure I was too."

"So you went to hurry him up, and found his body?"

"I waited as long as I dared but then thought, if I shouted at him that she was coming back, I could get him out. " Margaret opened her eyes to find Tom offering her a cup of hot sweet tea. The Irish solution to every situation, coupled with a nice biscuit. She smiled at him weakly, and he patted her arm. It was such a fatherly, warm gesture, she felt a wave of gratitude and without thinking, she burst out, "I'll go mad if I don't talk to someone!"

"That's the ticket, pet. Tell me what's bothering you."

"It's -oh it's so embarrassing. Brian and Frances were nice to me at first. When I bought the cottage, both my parents had died and I'm an only child so I was grateful to them. They always seemed to be doing something kind - bringing in my bins from the kerb , taking in post for me. But it got so I couldn't go in or out of my front door without one of them lighting on me. It was hard to put my finger on it, but I felt like they were sneering at me, underneath. Frances in particular. She made comments about my clothes and hair, but wrapped up in "helpfulness." Then she started on about how lucky I was. I mean, I lost my parents and I have very little family. Yes I'm glad to have a roof over my head but I would give it all up to have my mam and dad back. I didn't feel "lucky." Frances made it sound like I'd won the lottery, inheriting a few bob from them!"

She inhaled sharply and continued, "But I was fine up until the point where Brian started making comments, about immigrants and foreigners, and he said that St. Malachy's was getting too many of them. Well, they're my kids, Mrs Moriarty. They're just lovely little children, with hardworking parents, and they don't deserve to be spoken about like that. I told him so and he was furious, said after everything he'd done for me and I was so ungrateful. It was horribly unpleasant. I made up my mind to ignore them after that and just keep my distance. I thought I had managed to break with them."

She put down her cup on the table, her hands beginning to shake. Dymphna smiled at her reassuringly. It was like poison being drawn from a wound; unpleasant but ultimately healing. "Until last week," Margaret continued. "He called to the door, and barged in the moment I opened it. There was no pretense at friendliness then, he was horrible. He said - oh dear, I need to tell you something first. When I was young and we lived in another part of the city, closer to town, the area could be a little rough. The girls in my school were mostly nice but there were a few who were wild. I liked them, and they seemed to like me. I wanted to hang out with them and I wanted them to see me as cool."

"Ah." Dymphna could see where this was going.

"I-I did some incredibly stupid things to impress them. They encouraged me but it was my own fault. I shoplifted once or twice and then I got bolder and started spraying graffiti on shops and houses, trespassing...the more I did, the more they applauded and cheered me on. I didn't even realize that they weren't joining in, just watching me do it. And of course, one day I got caught. " She blushed, a deep red stain across her cheeks. "I'm so embarrassed about all this, but I wasn't a bad kid honestly. I was just...lonely. The more outrageously I behaved the more they seemed to admire me. Eventually I got too cocky - I climbed over a wall, into the back of a pub and tried to nick some beer. The yard had CCTV cameras, and they could see me clearly. The Gardaí were called, they came to our house. My poor parents!" She choked back a fresh sob. "When I saw how upset they were...and I was ashamed of myself. They begged the officers not to arrest me, and the Gardaí went back to the Pub, spoke to the owners. When they heard I was only fourteen, and that my parents would pay for any losses, they took pity on me."

She looked Dymphna square in the eye. "I swear to you, I took that second chance in both hands and ran with it. I was determined to make my parents proud, show them I wasn't a bad kid. I worked hard, I went to university, and all I ever wanted since then was to be a teacher and work with children. I've never done a wrong thing since that night, until Brian turned up in my house threatening me. He knew the owners of the pub, you see. They had told him about the robbery, and then about letting me off the hook. He remembered the name and did a little digging when I moved in...I reckon he knew almost from the day I bought Wisteria Cottage.

"That sounds about right," Tom remarked bitterly, recalling the stories he'd heard at Eve's the night before. Dymphna flashed a warning glance at him and he resolutely shut his lips. Margaret hadn't even heard him, she was caught up in her own story.

"I thought all that was behind me, but he said - he said because I had hidden it from the school, they would fire me. All I have left is being a teacher. My parents were so proud, it made everything worthwhile for them. They were such gentle people, they never cared about money or prestige, just our little family. My mother was a nurse, Dad was a plasterer. They were hardworking decent people. I miss them so much. The thought of being fired -" She caught her breath in a sob. "All he wanted was the key, and I hoped that would be an end to it. He would get whatever he wanted in Kimberly Cottage and then leave me alone. I gave him the key and regretted it almost immediately."

Dymphna's dark, beady eyes flashed. "That obnoxious little sod. Oh, Margaret, you have been a prize eejit. I doubt the school cares about some misdeamour in your youth. If anything, they'd be proud of you turning things around. You were never charged, either. It's not even like there's a record of it, let alone a conviction. Why on earth didn't you tell someone? I would have given him what-for, for a start. Ronan Desmond is a cop, and considering how friendly the pair of you are, you must have known that even if we didn't." She shook her head in exasperation. "Why not confide in him?" "She couldn't," Tom said gently. "Precisely *because* they're close. I bet you thought he would never think the same about you if he knew?"

Margaret nodded. "He's a detective. And he's the nicest man ever, but he's awful straight-laced. He wouldn't understand."

Dymphna laughed. "You wouldn't say that if you saw the man in Eve Caulton's living room, listening to a bunch of auld bats subverting the course of justice. He's been sitting on evidence and letting civilians poke around, trying desperately to give you the time to speak up."

The girl blushed, and bit her lip. "Ronan? Did he really?"

"Really. And now you're going to reward his faith and tell him everything. With a bit of luck, he'll be able to explain away the delay in coming forward ~ we'll say you were terrified of Frances O'Reilly, or maybe that you were genuinely sick. It's very hard to disprove "shock," I'd say. Go cry on your GP's shoulder would be my advice, get a note to say you were too shook to think straight."

Both Tom and Margaret eyed her with admiration mixed with shock. Mrs. Moriarty was known as a law-abiding, upstanding, somewhat severe, elderly lady. This ruthless approach to truth and expediency required some mental gymnastics to accept. Dymphna seemed unaware of the effect she was producing.

"We'll get Ronan over as soon as he can, and you two will have a chat. If you like I'll explain things to him first but it would be better coming from you. I think he's earned that."

The young teacher looked scared but readily agreed. The hopeless look had faded and she already looked more like her old self.

"There's just one more thing I need to know," Dymphna added. "Why did you steal the keys back?"

"Ah." She hung her head. "I panicked. I thought they could easily be traced to me, I mean my fingerprints would be all over them for a start. They were on the floor beside him. I had some idea that I could wipe them clean. When Ms. Caulton walked in, I stuck them in my pocket without thinking and then I couldn't say anything about them because it looked even worse."

Tom was flooded with relief. At last, they were moving along. Jo Maguire's theories were taking on flesh and bones. But who actually did the evil deed and how on earth could they prove it?

Across the road in the Merrion Complex, Claudia was pondering that very question. She had quickly made friends with

Amanda , who was delighted to meet yet another interesting old lady. This one asked fewer questions, opting instead to stand and contemplate the view of the cafe across from Chique Chicks, the view of the boutique from the cafe and the array of brightly coloured scarves and wraps scattered throughout the store. Amanda accepted a box of nice, Belgian chocolates for her cooperation and dutifully inputted Claudia's number in her phone, in case anything turned up.

"Anything at all," Claudia instructed. "Even if it seems a bit daft, do let me know. I'm going to go now and think things over. Hang on in there, young lady. We'll crack this yet."

# Chapter 21

Greta clapped her hands in appreciation and the other women murmured their approval, as Dymphna recounted how Tom and she had persuaded Margaret to talk. "Ronan is in there now, talking to her. I only hope he has the sense to reassure her, not come down too hard on the girl."

"He'll be fine," Niamh Caulton sipped her coffee and eyed Tom over the rim of the cup. "When a man is interested in a woman, he won't let a little thing like perjury put him off. Sure, haven't we all baggage? A past mistake here, a snakey little ex of a husband there, we all have *something.* If the person is worth it, they'll persevere."

Eve stared sternly at her mother, willing her to hush up.

"Poor Margaret," she said, "I do feel sorry for her. What a horrible thing to do to someone, blackmailing them." "Lowest of the low," agreed Greta. "I did a video on a case a few years back, series of women being blackmailed by a Lothario. Horrible. None of them would go to the authorities, for fear of the details coming out. They were desperate."

"What happened?" Eve asked with interest.

"My viewers tracked him down, from an IP address and a chance reference to hare coursing. Turns out a group of concerned citizens appearing at your place of work can be life changing. Little rat coughed up all his "evidence" in the end in return for not getting his legs bent in the wrong direction." Her eyes twinkled good-naturedly and Eve tried not to wonder how much was true and how much was Greta winding her up. No one else seemed phased by Granny Goode's story, which was - yeah. Worrying. Hopefully Jo was able to keep her Granny on the straight and narrow most of the time...

"What happens now?" Tom asked.

"I don't know," Dymphna replied. "Ronan will have to report all this and I suppose, see if they can build a case against Frances. Or if we're wrong about her, whoever else they can make fit."

"Do you honestly think Frances is innocent?"

"I think she's the most likely, but...how can we know for sure? It's time for the Gardaí to do their job now."

"Ronan took the journal," Eve had been loath to part with it, but he had promised faithfully to have it copied and returned within the week. "Once I get it back I'll send it on to Seamus Farrell. He's invited us down to see his family research, if anyone is interested. I'm definitely going to take up his offer. It would be lovely to see the house Julia and Con lived in."

"Me too," Tom exclaimed. "That would be great, I love family history."

They grinned at each other, while the quartet of wise women exchanged amused glances.

"I'll miss the excitement," Niamh said, "But you're right. Ronan has all the information now, he won't want us trampling all over the place."

Only Claudia looked mutinous, but she didn't argue. If a Brigadier of the Irish Women's Brigade had something on her mind, she kept it to herself and pursued it to the end. She did acknowledge the hard work of her fellows, though. "We did a good job everyone. He would never have found about the jewel, or why Margaret gave the key to Brian, or a lot of things like that, without us."

Eve agreed, but there was part of her relieved by their decision to let things go. The ladies were fit and healthy and sharp, but running around in your eighties asking questions about a potential killer was not ideal. The thought of her mother in danger was bad enough, but she had grown fond of the others too. Time to get back to painting and building a new life.

"But we should all meet up still," She looked at the group. "I've become used to you all arriving in on me, bearing food."

"Absolutely!" Before everyone left, they made a tentative plan for the following week. Tom paused at the door, letting the others go ahead.

"Would you like to do lunch during the week?" He asked hopefully. "Drive out along the coast, maybe go for a walk on the beach?"

Eve didn't hesitate. The beauty of being fifty, she thought, you don't bother playing games when a nice person asked you out. She waved him off, conscious of a silly grin on her face but as he was also beaming ear to ear, she didn't care. She wandered into the kitchen but her guests had cleared up after themselves. Time to do some work, then. She had a lecture to prepare for the following week, and more emails to answer, all sales inquiries which would make her bank manager happy. She was surprised to see a reply from Lesley Dylan, and clicked it open. It was less vague than the previous correspondence and explained that the proposed artwork was for a surprise birthday present. The recipient loved flowers and nature and had expressed an interest in Eve's work. The writer was not artistic, and was not sure what to ask for, hence the lack of clarity. Could they possibly meet in person, to discuss the matter? "*I would be perfectly happy to buy an existing piece, if it suited, and would probably be better able to chose if I could actually look at the pieces with your help.*"

It was reasonable enough, if a bit inconvenient. She could redirect them to one of the Galleries currently selling her pieces, but the chance of a direct sale, without having to give away a hefty commission was extremely tempting. She composed a quick email, saying that she could show her latest pieces if they thought one might suit. There were at least three that Eve felt suited the brief, such as it was. In a flurry of messages, it was agreed that Lesley would call later that evening, between 7 and 9.

Eve turned with relief to her easel. A few tweaks were all that remained to finish her still life, the empty bowls left after her ice cream and berries treat with Tom. She smiled looking at it, both at the memory and because she knew it was a good piece. It was a happy painting, something that would remind the viewer of childhood pleasures, or holidays. Lifting the canvas from the easel to set it aside safely, she froze mid-turn. A glint of colour caught her eye, just a fragment, caught on the edge of the painting. It was almost invisible, or one might have overlooked it thinking it was a frayed edge, but Eve knew every brush stroke of her paintings. She placed the picture carefully on the tiny desk and looked closely. Caught on the edge was a fragment of gaudily patterned cloth. It rang a faint bell but she couldn't place it. Possibly nothing more than a bit of material that shed from a floaty scarf or a wrap. She wracked her brains thinking of anything similar that had been worn by her friends but drew a blank. "I'm being silly." She chided herself. "Leave it along for now and lift it off later."

Eve turned her attention to picking a few pieces for her new client.

Across the road in the Merrion Complex, Amanda waited impatiently for her boss to stop fussing over the stock.

"We have it all in hand, Mrs. O'Reilly." the girl said politely. "Everything is priced, and the stock lists are up to date. I can manage on my own until Nora gets in."

Frances sniffed. "Hmm. I suppose so. Watch that Nora, she is as lazy as sin. If she thinks she can get away with it, she'll be on her phone all day."

Amanda gritted her teeth. Nora was a nice, hardworking girl and didn't deserve that. There was no point arguing with Frances, though. She simply wouldn't listen. With a bit of luck, it wouldn't be for too much longer. She had applied for any number of jobs in the city centre the previous evening, including a boutique recommended by that nice Mrs. Warren. Her mother had been genuinely pleased when she described how she had been "hanselled." It was an old tradition, her mother said, and it was considered lucky. Amanda had decided that it was a sign to go out and make her own luck. Any job would be better than working for the permanently unimpressed Frances.

At last, her employer left for the rest of the day and Amanda was free to rearrange the stock back into its proper place. It drove her mad to see the pieces placed so that no one could see the prices or the patterns properly. Especially the scarves. Frances had been faffing around with them all day, fussing and reorganizing. And look! She tutted in annoyance. There was one on the bottom that looked crumpled, with its sale tags missing and a frayed edge. How careless! She furrowed her brow trying to recall - yes, it was exactly like one Frances had worn earlier in the week. If only Frances would stop "borrowing" her own stock and then putting it back. No one would want that piece now, and when it was left unsold, guess who would get the blame?

To her dismay, directly under that one was another scarf, crumpled and showing signs of having been worn. It was at least undamaged, but like the first one it was missing its tags. Amanda considered both garments carefully, thinking, "How odd. Two of the same pattern." She wondered, why two?

Stepping out into Bramble Lane, Ronan hugged Margaret, a slightly awkward hug but full of promise. He was conscious of a huge sense of relief. At no point had he seriously considered her in the role of calculated, cold blooded killer but he had definitely wondered if she could have done it in a moment of panic. The detective in him could see she was lying, but the thought of cross examining her, interrogating it out of her, made his heart ache. Hearing the story from her own lips, voluntarily, had set his mind at rest. There was a ring of truth about her story now, and he welcomed it.

He knew that his partner, Cullen, would understand. He'd already discreetly hinted that Ronan might need to persuade Margaret to come in.

"We can only hold off so long, Ronan. I'll do what I can but you know yourself, it looks bad."

Now, thanks to Bramble Lane's peculiar brand of neighbour-hood watch, he was armed with the outline of a statement and ready to make the case in favour of Margaret. He glanced around as he returned to his car. Only Eve's car was in her drive-way. Dymphna was probably off with her grandchildren. Tom could be anywhere, the man was a great one for outings and joining clubs. He had told Ronan once that he was determined to say yes to everything, try to live a bit before it was too late. He had been a good friend to Margaret, Ronan thought. Making a mental note to buy the man a pint at the earliest opportunity he got into his car and hit speed dial for Cullen's number.

It was a long day all round, the ladies having such a lot to catch up on. Visits, meetings, household and garden chores, things that had been set aside to concentrate on the Kimberly Cottage case all clamoured for attention. Since he returned to the Merrion Garda station, Garda Detective Desmond joined his colleague Cullen in pouring over evidence. This included some very interesting CCTV footage from cameras overlooking the main road, the Bramble Lane junction and footage from a private security camera set up in a back garden that overlooked the back of the Bramble Lane cottages. In Wisteria Cottage Margaret Furey ate a proper meal for the first time in almost a week and decided to have a lie down. It had been equally long since she had been able to close her eyes more than half an hour at a time. She fell into a deep, dreamless nap. Tom returned home from a very enjoyable meeting of the local drama society, where he was a dead cert to play the older leading man in the next production. He glanced at Kimberly as he passed and wondered if Eve might be persuaded to join in. They could use a lady for mature roles, or even a good artistic eye to help with scenery and so forth. He was smiling as he let himself in.

The O'Reilly residence was dark and quiet, with no sign of Frances' car. If anyone had been watching it, in the early evening gloom, it certainly looked as if its owner was away.

Claudia was at home, not far from Bramble Lane, in one of the large, red-bricked Victorian Villas on a tree-lined avenue off the Main Merrion Road. She sat in front of a fire, allowing the modest blaze to warm her legs and letting her mind drift. She felt sure she had grasped the right thread, so to speak, and now she just needed to unravel it one knot at a time. She let her mind drift, passing over the last few days, all the pieces of information and little snippets. She saw the girl, Amanda, standing in the boutique. Serving customers, keeping one eye on the window because her boss was sitting in the cafe opposite, in full view. How odd, to sit so obviously. Making sure everyone could see her. Dressed in the uniform of the glamourous, Dublin matron. Blonde hair, a fancy scarf, the blouses and cardigans that looked so gaudy to Claudia but were fashionable now, she supposed.

If you thought about it, one woman looked much like another when they dressed like that. "Uniform" was the right description. You could easily mistake one coiffured blonde for another. Like Liza Dunne and Frances O'Reilly. So very similar, especially from a distance...

Her phone rang, and "Nice Amanda" popped up on the screen. Talk of the divil, Claudia thought but she answered it readily.

"Mrs. Warren?"

"Yes, Amanda? Is everything okay?"

"Yes, well - I'm not sure. You said to call if anything odd happened."

"And it has?"

"I think so. I was sorting some scarfs today, some expensive ones. They're Mrs. O'Reilly's favourites. She had messed them all up, moved them from their usual place. It means they won't sell, she knows this but she will go moving stock anyway. It's a total pain. But sure, anyway, I put them back as soon as she's out of the place. I was moving this lot and noticed there were two of the at the bottom, all crumpled and off their hangers.

The tags are off them too. And one has a slightly damaged edge, like it caught on something. I know it sounds trivial but...I'm fairly sure that's the type of scarf she was wearing the day of the Murder. It's very eye-catching, if you know what I mean."

Claudia recalled the type of accessory Frances stocked and shuddered. "Yes, I know exactly what you mean."

"Now that I'm saying it to you, it seems ridiculous. But I thought I should let you know."

"Quite right! It's very interesting and I think, important. Do me a favour, take them and put them into a clean plastic bag. A zip-lock bag or one that can be sealed."

"I'm way ahead of you," Amanda sounded very pleased with herself. "I put both of them into two stock bags, they're sealed up and hidden away safely in the shop.We don't shut until eight tonight. "

"Good girl. What is it now...seven fifteen. I'll be there in fifteen minutes. I think you may have just supplied the last thing we needed."

# Chapter 22

"It's very simple, when you think about it. She couldn't afford to be absent during the time of the murder and of course, she knew when that would be because she bullied Brian into breaking in this afternoon, even though it was a huge risk. She couldn't have known Eve would go out for a walk, so she told Brian to bring a knife and I'm very much afraid the idea was for Brian to kill Eve if necessary."

"I think that explains the second, clean knife. I'll get back to that in a moment. What I am sure about, is how she faked an alibi."

Detectives Desmond and Cullen exchanged uncertain glances. Claudia tutted at the pair and held up a scarf to demonstrate her point. It had taken some effort to persuade the pair to meet her at Chique Chicks, but they had come and now she had to explain her theory. Garda Jo Maguire listened intently but let the detectives take the lead. Every now and then, she gave Claudia encouraging nods.

Amanda had double checked to make sure Frances wasn't in the building, and now watched with interest as Claudia draped herself in finery and headed out the door, into the shopping centre corridor. "Okay, boys. I'll walk around and you tell me what you see when I come back."

She strode up the hallway, her sensible shoes with their sturdy heels echoing in the near empty shopping centre. The men watched her walk out of sight, around the corner before reappearing and walking halfway back towards them. She then turned sharply, walked out of sight again, reappeared and re-entered the store. "So, Gentlemen, what did you see?"

"You walked out, turned left, disappeared from view, walked back into view, turned again halfway down, walked out of view and then back into view, whereupon you returned to the starting point, that would here." Detective Cullen recited promptly. "I still don't get it."

"What if I told you, you are wrong. That you did not, in fact, see me do what you've just described?"

"With all due respect, Missus, I'd say you were taking the mickey."

Amanda frowned, but Claudia didn't seem to be a bit put out.

"Aha! Well, now, be prepared to eat your words." She put two fingers in her mouth and gave a piercing whistle that echoed off the marble and glass of the shop and up the corridor, causing several last minute shoppers to jump in fright. At this signal, another "Claudia" appeared and wafted down towards the boutique, scarves flowing behind her. Cullen frowned, his mouth open, while comprehension began to dawn on Ronan's face. "Oh my," he breathed, "You clever old bird." Amanda coughed reprovingly. "Sorry," he said to Claudia, "But you are clever."

Cullen stared at the second version of the Brigadier. His face was comical when he looked closely and realized he was looking at a smaller woman, built on much slighter lines, although she had bulked up with coats and woollens to resemble Claudia's more substantial shape. "Hi!" Niamh Caulton grinned.

Cullen suddenly laughed. "So that's it, that's how she had an alibi?"

"That's how she did it. Earlier that day, she insisted Amanda take an early lunch, with no rush to get back on time. She closed the shop as soon as Amanda left, ran across to Bramble Lane, knowing Amanda would see her car in its usual parking space in the employees car park. She had a few things she needed to do, to ensure her plan worked and she got them done hours before the murder could possibly take place. She went home, out into her back garden and moved along the back of the houses until she reached Kimberly Cottage. It wouldn't have been easy, but not too hard for a relatively young, fit woman. She got over the fence into Eve's back garden, and she opened the back door with Maud Williams' missing backdoor key. A key she didn't tell Brian about. I fear Frances had planned this for a very long time, at least in theory. At some point Brian was going to get into Kimberly and search it and she wanted to be ready. She left the back door unlocked, ready for the afternoon's antics."

"Then she went for her own lunch. She dressed in a scarf from her own inventory, a very noticeable item. Her whole outfit was carefully chosen, as was her hair colour, and the set of her hair. She copied it all from Liza Dunne, you see. And she persuaded Liza to eat lunch in full view of her staff, dressed in an identical outfit and then meet her in the centre's toilets to change. Just like Niamh here, Liza looked the part well enough that anyone asked would agree she was Frances. Niamh isn't even much like me, while that pair are quite alike in build and height."

"At the end of the hour, they meet in the public toilers. Liza emerges from the bathroom in her own clothes, Francis returns to work as if she's never left the place, and Amanda is convinced her employer was never out of her sight. But I couldn't shake the feeling that it had to be wrong. Liza left and went to the toilet block on the first floor. That bothered me. Why not go to the one in the café?"

Ronan answered. "Because she had to meet Frances, make sure that only one Frances O'Reilly was seen going back to the shop."

Cullen whistled admiringly. "Some nerve, all the same."

"She is a very resourceful, ruthless woman. And she is a bitter one at that. Liza Dunne, for all her faults, is convinced Frances is her bosom buddy. I bet she's a bit shaken that she provided an unwitting alibi for a murder but even now, thinks it was just an awful coincidence that the murder happened on the very day she impersonated her friend."

All four of them took a moment to pity the easily duped Liza.

"So, this is enough, yes? You can at least search her house on the back of this?"

Ronan considered. "We can apply for a warrant, yes. I think it's enough. I hope so, anyway."

"So do I," Claudia replied. "Let's hope she's not up to anything in the meantime."

# Chapter 23

Eve was pleased with the selection of paintings she had pulled from storage. Her new one, titled "Afters," she placed out in the tiny utility room. Somehow, she didn't want that one to catch a buyer's eye. It had struck her that Tom might appreciate it, a reminder of his favourite treat. She held up one of her floral works to the light and eyed it critically. It was a very classic Eve Caulton piece, probably the safest for someone without much knowledge to buy, and definitely should make the recipient happy if they were a fan.

A knock at the door made her jump and she checked her watch. Seven thirty, already. That had to be Lesley, come to view the art. She opened the door with a warm smile and paused. A figure greeted her, rather swamped in a large overcoat with a scarf around her face and a woollen hat jammed on low on the head.

"Lesley?" Eve asked uncertainly.

In reply the figure nodded, then without waiting to be invited in, pushed past her and into the living room.

Eve stared at the person, still swathed in black scarves and coat. They stood with their back to her, face turned away, but she felt there was something vaguely familiar about the figure. She gave herself a little mental shake, and reminded herself that the sale of a painting would go a long way towards paying that month's bills. If the buyer was a bit pushy or rude, it was just something to put up with. "Lesley?" She asked again and received a nod in reply. Eve shut the front door and gestured to the living room. "Won't you step in?"

Lesley moved into the room and slowly began to unwind the layers of scarves. "I've pulled out a few paintings I thought you might like, for your friend." Eve pointed at the display she'd set up on the couch and easel. "Would you like a cup of tea or coffee? I'll pop the kettle on."

As she walked into the kitchen it struck her, she had no idea if "Lesley" was a guy or a girl. Not that it mattered, except if she had thought about it she wouldn't have arranged to meet a strange man in her home at night. It was silly though, the chances were her visitor just wanted to buy a picture and go on their way. She peeked out into the living room and was reassured to see a woman with rather coarse dark hair, worn in shoulder length waves, and wearing a dark skirt and jacket over a more colourful blouse. Considerably more colourful and quite familiar.

Eve poured hot water into her best china teapot, the match of her tea set that was already on the tray. It had a poppy theme, with the cheerful red flowers painted around the bottom half of each cup, jug, and the teapot, and poppies around the rim of each plate and saucer. It wasn't unlike the pattern on her visitor's blouse, Eve realized in amusement. Now, where had she seen a motif like that recently, she asked herself. Very eye catching, but nicer by far on her china than on - on Frances' O'Reilly's blouse! Standing on her doorstep earlier that day.

Frances was in her living room, in a disguise. Eve drew a deep breath and tried not to panic. She weighed up the options.

It was Murphy's Law, but her mobile phone was in the living room, on the bookshelves instead of in here with her. It might be possible to make her way over to it, grab it discreetly and text someone. She wracked her brains for anything she could do in the meantime, to attract attention. Her eyes fell on the back door key and she slipped it into the lock. Very quietly she turned the key and opened the door. Immediately a slice of light from the kitchen cut across the dark of the garden. If Dymphna Moriarty looked out at all, assuming she had returned home from her outing, she would notice. "I could just slip out and try to get over the back fence," Eve considered. But there was no guarantee she could clamber over the wooden structure, fit at fifty didn't necessarily include being nimble enough to shimmy up 6 feet of smooth pine. And there was something in her that baulked at running away. She thought about arming herself with a knife, eyeing the sharp edged vegetable knife. What would she do with it though? Never in her life had Eve wielded a weapon with the intention of hurting another human being. Would she even be able to use it?

On the other hand, that was Frances O'Reilly out there in her living room. Eve slipped the knife into her trousers pocket and hoped she wouldn't end up stabbing herself through the thigh. Picking up her tray and fixing a smile on her face, she bustled back into the living room, careful to give no hint of recognition to her unwelcome visitor.

"Well, have you seen anything you like?" She asked brightly.

"Lesley" aka Frances, kept her head down and pretended to be engrossed in the details of "*Meadow at Dawn*," a riot of wildflowers and summer skies that Eve had painted that summer.

"Oh, that's a nice one," Eve encouraged. "One of my

favourites, if I'm allowed to say that about my own work. But I feel I truly captured the light and the atmosphere of the place – a field down beyond in Wexford, a farmer has turned over to wildflowers for the bees." As she babbled, she moved closer to the bookshelf, until the phone was within arm reach. "Although the second one there, "*Violets,*" might be nearer to the ones your friend would have seen in the media."

She casually reached behind her and palmed the phone, keeping it out of Frances' line of sight. She glanced down, and to her dismay, saw the battery symbol at four percent. It wouldn't last long enough for a phone call. She would be lucky to get it to send a text.

"Do you know?" Eve had a desperate flash of inspiration. "I'm sure I have a catalogue somewhere here, with pictures of the last exhibition in it, might help to show you." She turned her back, opened messages at the first name – Tom MacDonagh as it happened – and frantically typed "Help. F in my house. SOS" and punched send just as the screen went blank and the phone died. There was no way of knowing if the message had even gone. She swallowed hard, grabbed a catalogue from a recent gallery show and waved it triumphantly. "Here we are, I think. Would you like to see?"

Her guest was carefully examining the edge of the paintings now. She wore gloves, Eve noted, close fitting leather that fitted snugly.

"Are these your most recent?" the voice was gruff and pitched deeper than Frances' usual speech, but Eve recognized the sharp tone. "Yes, they're the ones," Some instinct told her to lie. "Afters" was safely out of view, and if for some reason the lethal widow wanted to see it, that was good enough reason to keep it away from her. There was a sigh from the other woman, and she straightened up.

"What about the one you were working on?" Frances didn't bother to disguise her voice this time. "Come on now. Where is it? You had a blank canvas on this easel. Give it to me."

Eve squared up to her neighbour, looking her directly in the eye. Now she could see her clearly, she saw with a shock that the hair was a rough wig, the kind you see on mannequins. It struck her that Frances had raided her boutique for the props to her disguise, and a bubble of inappropriate laughter fought with the sheer terror of being alone with the killer.

"Would you not take that thing off your head?" Her voice sounded calm and collected, to Eve's surprise.

"What?" Frances touched the wig with one gloved hand. "This? No, no. This stays put until I leave. No one will be able to say they saw me, because I haven't been here. They'll find emails from Lesley Dylan, on an IP address that will trace back to Liza Dunne. And any description will match your husband's new wife as easily as me. She has a selection of wigs, did you know that? She fancies herself as a fashionista. Hah! She tells people she took me under her wing, do you know that? As if I've ever needed fashion advice from the likes of her. All hoighty toighty, high and mighty now, but it's far from designer labels she was reared. Liza Murphy, that's how she started life and not around here either."

Eve smiled carefully. "But you're the one with the boutiques, not Liza. Why would you need fashion tips from her?"

"Exactly! You can see it so why can't those snooty auld bats in the Brigade? Liza telling them ridiculous stories about lending me clothes and introducing me to her stylist. But they're all the same, these women."

"Cliques," Eve murmured sympathetically. "It's not what

you know, it's who you know. Liza can splash a lot of cash, and Peter is well-connected. That's all it takes around here. Whereas a hard working, clever woman is completely over-looked."

"Yes! Thank you, someone finally sees it." Frances clapped her hands. "It's so frustrating. But Liza is so stupid, she agreed to pose as me, without even asking questions. Isn't that gas? I told her I wanted to check out something my staff were up to, and she just agreed."

"You wouldn't have been so gullible," Eve agreed.

"You know it! Ah well, it worked out well for me. Now, I need that other canvas. I caught my scarf on it, you see. Almost knocked the easel over, trying to get past. It was Margaret's fault, barging in like that. Couldn't even hold her nerve and stay in her house for a half hour. I saw her coming, thank heavens, or she'd have caught me red-handed. It would have been easier in some ways, if I'd dealt with her there and then. You can't plan for everything though, can you?"

She slipped her hand in her pocket and it emerged clutching a long sharp knife with a wicked looking edge. It flashed and glinted as she took sudden steps towards Eve.

"I'm sorry about this," the widow said quite politely. "You're a bit brighter than most of them, but honestly, I just can't risk any more loose ends. Where's that canvas?"

"It's gone," Eve said. "I used it for another painting, and yes, there was a rough edge with some fabric on it. But I took the fabric off it and threw it out. How could I know it was yours? It's long gone."

Frances tilted her head and stared hard at Eve. "No. You're lying to me. I bet it's here somewhere. Where is it, Eve? Don't try my patience any longer or I'll just deal with you now, take my chances of finding it."

A vision of her mother, years before, repeating patiently, "It's all about visualizing, Eve. You decide what you need to happen and you create it in your mind." The painting would be safe, the evidence on it would remain hidden from view. Frances won't be able to see it, Eve told herself. It wouldn't exist for her; she will overlook it. She seized on one thought like a mantra, "It's totally in the dark and she can't see it."

"There's only one other painting here," Eve pointed at the small room off the main living room. She took a few steps away from Frances, getting the small sofa between them. "Go on, see for yourself."

"You first,"

"Why? So you can stab me in the back?"

"If you don't, I'll stab you through the eye," the woman gave a grim little smile.

Eve weighed her options and shrugged.

"Alright then," She moved quickly to the connecting door, keeping as much distance between them as she could. "Look!" When she flicked the light switch, nothing happened. The room remained dark, not a flicker of light came from the bulb.

"Oh. Well, look anyway."

She stepped back and pointed into the little storeroom. Frances edged past her keeping the knife held tight.

"Where? I can't see it. You fool, where is it?"

Without warning something small and slightly furry with bright dark eyes shrieked out of the darkness and wrapped itself around the murderous neighbour's face. She gave a muffled scream and flailed wildly grabbing at the small rodent with wings.

"Whassampppph!"

Eve moved out of the way of the knife and grabbed Frances' arm firmly. "HELP!" She screamed at the top of her voice, kicking and punching the arm in an attempt to dislodge the knife. "Help me!"

The bat had moved up Frances' face and was busy scratching at her forehead and hairline, making the ugly wig sit askew on her head. Eve would have laughed if it wasn't so deathly serious.

"Get it off me!" Frances wailed. "Get it off." She wrenched her arm clear of Eve's hold and the knife swung forward, missing Eve by a hair's breadth and nicking the tiny mammal on one wing. With a little scream of pain, it let go and fluttered back into the dark. There was a muffled bump, but Eve could only hope it was okay. She had her hands full wrestling Frances who was now more anxious to escape than anything else. Eve grasped the vegetable knife hidden in her pocket, pulling it out and sticking it in the fleshy top part of her assailant's arm. The little knife didn't do a lot of damage, before it slipped from her grasp, but Frances screeched, and stopped struggling. Eve gave one more good thump to the arm, and the other woman dropped her weapon, pushed roughly past Eve and made for the back door.

Her way out was blocked by Tom, armed with a garden shears. "Oh no you don't!" he roared. She screamed again and cursed roundly, spinning on her heel and crashing through the living room, into the hallway and wrenching open the front door.

"Gotcha," said Ronan Desmond, his face hard and angry. He grabbed the woman and turned her expertly, restraining her arms behind her back as Jo Maguire produced handcuffs. "Frances O'Reilly I'm arresting you on suspicion of murdering your husband, Brian O'Reilly..." She struggled and shouted abuse but it was no use. The long arm of the law had her in its grip and from the satisfied look on Ronan's face, it was not planning on letting go anytime soon.

"Eve?" Claudia's anxious face bobbed in and out of view behind the two cops, followed by Niamh. "Eve, are you alright?"

"I'm fine," Eve replied, "But I think Dymphna needs a doctor." Her neighbour emerged from the dark store room clutching her arm, bright red showing through her light tan cardigan. "I'm all right, Dear," Dymphna replied calmly. As she passed Eve, she gave a tiny wink. "She only managed to wing me."

Claudia rolled her eyes.

# Chapter 24

The next few hours passed in a blur of making statements, retelling the evening's events over and over, seeing Dymphna's arm patched up by a very handsome paramedic, snatching a hurried conference with Garda Jo Maguire and promising to all meet up the moment everyone was free. Niamh and Greta volunteered to wait at the station and escort the others to Kimberly, leaving Tom free to drive himself and Eve home to Bramble Lane. Now Eve sat in an armchair, having poured Tom and herself a large brandy. Neither had to ask the other how they felt. She was conscious of a deep gratitude to Dymphna, but she knew the sight of Tom armed with a garden tool, disheveled from climbing over the wooden fence and ready to do battle - that was the memory she would cherish.

For his part, Tom was conscious of having acquitted himself well. He was also relieved to his very core that Eve had escaped unharmed. He sipped his brandy and promised himself that he would take very good care of his charming neighbour from now on. An hour passed by quickly, the companionable silence punctuated by brief chats.

"I suppose the others will be here soon," Tom stretched and settled himself again. "Sure, even Ronan Desmond must be running out of questions by now."

Eve chuckled. "He's delighted with himself, you can tell. The murder has been solved, the killer's in custody and Margaret is largely off the hook."

"I'm glad for them. Young people deserve happiness. Older people too, of course."

Eve turned her head to hide a blush. "We all deserve a bit of joy."

"Be the hokey, though!" Tom slapped the arm of the sofa. "We forgot about the jewel."

Eve laughed at the old-fashioned exclamation but agreed, "It must be somewhere in Frances' house, or at least I hope so. I think Jo was right, she must have grabbed it and run, stuffing the box back into the cubbyhole and closing it up. If you think about it, that's where the easel was standing. She must have snared her scarf on the edge in her rush."

"I'd love to be there when they find the jewellery," Tom's expression was wistful. "I suppose we have to wait for the Gardaí to find it. There's still some bits I don't fully understand, though. Claudia seems to have been the one who figured stuff out."

"You can ask her yourself," Eve said, pointing out the window. "There they are, that's Mam's car."

Niamh was first through the door, determined to hug her daughter and fuss over her. Eve let her; she knew if either Mairead or Liam had been in danger for even a moment she would have felt the same. She hugged her back, accepted a cup of tea so strong the spoon could have stood up in it, and so sweet her teeth hurt. Niamh insisted she put a wrap around her shoulders and a cushion behind her back and then, running out of things to fuss over, the overwrought Irish Mother sat on the sofa and had a short cry. Everyone else busied themselves making tea and producing cakes and fussing over Dymphna with her injury. Tom gave up his seat to one of the ladies and carried in a kitchen chair. By the time Jo Maguire arrived, still in uniform but with her cap off and top buttons undone, a comfortable scene greeted her. "Oh, pour us a cup of tea, I'm gasping!" She sank into the last space on the sofa and wriggled until she got comfortable. "Thank you. And a slice of that carrot cake. Sure, throw a slice of that tea brack on it too. Excellent. Now, who wants to start? Tell me everything, Eve. I was there when Claudia showed us the trick Frances pulled to get an alibi and I've heard bits and pieces down in the station but I'm dying to hear everything!"

Where to start, was the question. "You go first, Claudia." Eve said. "I haven't heard any of that yet."

Claudia was delighted to kick off the story. She gave a colourful but succinct account of her deductions and the demonstration Niamh and she had given in Chique Chicks boutique. "Truth be told, that girl Amanda deserves the praise," she concluded modestly. "If she hadn't rung me, it might have been days before it clicked. And then, where would we be? As it was, it took a bit of persuasion to get the detectives to listen, and we have Jo here to thank for that. She made them come."

"Ah here! I couldn't make them. I just...put it to them in the right way," Jo demurred. In reality she had hinted broadly that letting a bunch of senior citizens solve a murder under their noses would reflect poorly on the Merrion branch of the force. "So, Amanda realized two scarves had been used and replaced? Did Frances put them there because she thought it was clever - hidden in full view?"

"Probably put them back to sell, according to Amanda.

Frances is as mean as Scrooge."

"Either way, once I knew there were two scarves, it became clear. I could see it in my mind's eye. Two women, two outfits, two scarves. And coupled with Liza Dunne being so shifty about it all, the plan just clicked into place for me."

"What I don't understand is the two knives? I get her hiding it because it was so distinctive, but why did she have both of them that day?"

"Ah. This I can help with." Jo cast a sympathetic glance at Eve. "This won't be easy to hear but this is what we think happened. Frances was not going to leave anything to chance. She had spent two weeks or probably longer, plotting how to kill Brian but make it look like he was killed stopping a robbery. The cottage was supposed to be empty. For the fortnight they were away, she worked on Brian until he agreed to get the keys from Margaret, and enter the cottage on that precise afternoon. Before they went on holiday she had lined up Liza with a cock and bull tale of wanting to catch her employees out, being lazy or taking unauthorized breaks or something daft. Then disaster struck, and they arrived home to find Eve in possession of Kimberly Cottage."

"That's when she tweaked the plan. Brian took one knife with him and was prepared to dispatch Eve if she got in his way. As we learned from his cousins, that jewel had become an obsession with him, much as it had been for his ancestor William. While he searched and using his family knowledge, found the jewel – Frances sneaked in the back door and stabbed him. If things had gone the way she hoped, she would have turned the place over to look as if burglars had struck and then slipped away, taking Brian's knife with her. She had only started to stage the scene however, when Margaret arrived."

"And the rest is history, as we say in the business," Greta finished. "The rest is history," agreed her granddaughter.

Eve took up the story at this point, recounting how "Lesley Dylan" had tricked her into an evening sales meeting. "So gullible of me, I can hardly believe it. It was just such a typical email though, I get so many like it I didn't even question it. People are always asking for special attention, one to one meetings. It sounded vague, annoying and demanding. A typical client, which is why so many artists only deal through agents." "When I realized it was Frances, I couldn't think what to do, except try to attract someone's attention by leaving the back door wide open."

"And it worked," her neighbour replied. "It caught my eye almost immediately. The light from the kitchen was like a beacon, I realized immediately something was wrong."

Tom shook his head. "You were extremely brave, Dymphna, but you're lucky you didn't break your neck climbing over the back wall. It was foolhardy, it truly was. And tackling that woman head on, it's a wonder all you got was a flesh wound on your arm."

Eve and Dymphna carefully avoided eye contact. "I'm hardier than I look, Tom MacDonagh. I can still climb a ladder, you know. It's not that hard. And all I did was startle her. It was Eve who grabbed her arm and started belting her."

Jo sniggered. Her eyes dancing in her head with suppressed mischief, she said,

"Do you know what Frances claims? You won't believe it but she says a bat attacked her. Hickey, the big gom, asked her, "Are you calling that poor sweet old woman a bat?" He was outraged, like. Then she says no, an actual bat, and asked for a rabies shot."

195

"She's not the full shilling," Tom said solemnly, then frowned as the others started laughing. He was sure there was a joke he just wasn't getting but sure, didn't the women like a joke at a man's expense now and then? He grinned around at them all. They were a lovely bunch of ladies, in his opinion.

"So that's it," Eve shook her head. "I can hardly believe it's over." "There's only one thing left," Tom reminded them. "It's the antique dealer in me but I can't wait to hear when - if - they find the jewel. Or whatever it was that was so precious, it was worth killing for."

"Ah, I forgot," Jo sprang to her feet and checked her watch. "Ronan - Detective Desmond, I should say - asked that you all meet here, around eight in the morning. We're going to do a full search. If that blasted gem is there, he's determined to find it. He thought ye might like to be in at the finish and get to see what happens."

"I'll be there, anyway," Tom promised, his eyes lighting up. "I think we can all agree, nothing would keep us away. Let's get some sleep and meet here in the morning, Jo can text when they want us down."

It took a while to clear the living room, between Niamh's reluctance to leave her daughter alone overnight and Tom hovering solicitously in the background, equally loathe to leave Eve. She finally shooed them out, promising to text one or both should she feel even slightly scared. At last, there was only Dymphna left and Eve helped her on with her coat, easing it gently over the injured arm.

"I'm going to walk you home, and see you settled," Eve announced firmly, "But first you're going to explain something. I saw a bat. In an otherwise empty room. Like, even with the light off, it's not a big enough room for you to hide in. Then there was no bat, and there was only you, and -" Her neighbour held up her good hand, to cut her off.

"You know fine well, Eve Caulton. You don't need me to spell it out. Just like you know why the lights didn't come on. Don't pretend you don't." Her dark eyes flashed, but there was no unkindness in them, or in her tone of voice. "But if you ever want to discuss *how* to do these things, I'm just next door. Now, help me home, like a good woman."

# Chapter 25

At half past eight the following morning, Jo texted the group message thread. Everyone was waiting in Eve's cottage, enjoying breakfast when her summons came. "Come now!"

No one needed a second invitation. They were outside the O'Reilly home in minutes, where Jo's colleague Garda Hickey ushered them inside with a slightly grumpy air. Garda Maguire was in the thick of the investigation and he was outside playing bouncer to a group of sightseers. He wondered, not for the first time, how Jo managed it.

The two detectives greeted them warmly, Cullen shaking Tom's hand, asking Dymphna about her injuries and all but saluting Claudia for whom he seemed to have formed a doglike devotion. Eve had never been inside the O'Reillys but wasn't surprised that they had stuffed the cottage with modern furniture, fine in its own way but totally unsuitable for the old place. She took her place on one of the rigid, awkwardly shaped chairs around a chrome and glass coffee table with a sort of futuristic, twisted, tabletop. It looked interesting but a teapot would slide right off it.

"We found it," Ronan said without preamble. "Now, it's not regulation to have you lot in here, but in fairness, we owe you one. So, in the spirit of neighbourly goodwill, we thought you'd like to see the end of the story." He produced a small plastic box, the kind people put snacks into for toddlers, with snap clips to close it. Pulling them open and removing the lid, the detective upturned the container and emptied the contents into his palm. Holding out his hand for everyone to see, he unveiled a handful of gold and gems. A delicate gold chain held a necklace of small golden flowers, set with white diamonds and tiny emerald chips. A matching bracelet and earrings set nestled beside it, all of them exquisitely wrought and even to an untrained eye, of the highest quality.

But the star of the show was undoubtedly the large pendant held on a long gold chain, the pendant being a gold circle holding a dark, red stone. "That's a ruby," breathed Tom. "Absolutely superb. Perfect."

Ronan nodded. "We've been in touch with the Farrells, Seamus remembers his grandmother describing some of her mother's jewellery. There's no doubt. This is what she hid, and promised to her brother William. if he signed over Kimberly Cottage."

"But - but she could have sold it and bought the cottage three times over. Four, possibly," Tom objected.

"She could have sold it and saved her daughter from a life of toil and insecurity," Niamh pointed out. "She was some selfish wagon."

They all gazed at the treasure for a few moments more, but the memory of what that Mrs. O'Reilly had been willing to sacrifice to hold onto the baubles had robbed them of some of their beauty. "Julia was right to get away. Look at the life she had with Con, the good they did. All those things have brought is misery."

Ronan wrapped up the haul, and placed it in an evidence bag. "Well, they belong to someone now, either the William O'Reilly side or the Julia Farrells. The lawyers will have to sort that out." "Oh I do hope they don't fall out over them," Eve replied. "Both sets of cousins seem so nice now, it would be a pity if it all flared up again. I suppose Julia was her daughter, and she was left the Cottage with its contents."

"Yeah, but you're forgetting. Her mother promised it to Uncle William. He upheld his end of the bargain when he signed over Kimberly Cottage." Claudia pointed out.

"Ah but there's nothing in writing to say it was contingent on receiving the jewellery," Greta pointed out.

"We have to get Jennie Warren on the case," Eve laughed. "Or we'll all end up fighting about it."

They trooped back to Kimberly Cottage and tucked into the feast of a breakfast that had been keeping warm in the oven.

"It's over now," Eve thought. Frances was safely locked up and there were no more mysteries. It struck her that it had been just a week since she moved in, which seemed impossible. Bramble Lane and its residents felt so close to her now. Despite all that had happened, she felt at home here. She had fielded frantic calls from Mairead and Liam since early morning, and she knew they were appalled at her wanting to stay in Kimberly Cottage. "Mam, for goodness sake, first a murder and then a hostage situation. You should come stay with me for a few weeks, house hunt again.." Mairead in particular wanted to swoop in and "rescue" her mother. "I will do no such thing," Eve had laughed at her. "I love this cottage and honestly, considering all that's happened it's probably the safest house in Dublin now. Lightning hardly strikes twice, now does it. Besides, I've got to know all my neighbours now and isn't one of them a Garda detective?" Mairead remained unconvinced. She rang off but not before announcing, "I'm coming to visit next weekend and I'm bringing Liam. I'll see for myself."

Eve sidled up to Tom and asked him would he like to come round for his dinner on Friday? Her kids were coming over and she wanted them to see that not all her neighbours were homicidal.

Some men might think it far too soon to meet her family, but not Tom. He whispered a silent thank you to his lovely Carol, whom he was sure had a hand in sending Eve his way. He had promised her he would live and say "yes" to every opportunity. "I'd be delighted," he said.

Mairead and Liam did visit but somehow by the end of their weekend stay had changed their minds about their mother's new home. They both thoroughly approved of Tom. The presence of a detective nearby did much to assuage Mairead's fears. Liam was happy to see his mother looking well and full of plans. He went so far as to volunteer his services to help Tom make raised beds for the back garden and showed an interest in the difficulties of growing pest free organic vegetables. They soon stopped fussing over her and instead allowed her to pamper them. A thoroughly successful weekend all round.

Bramble Lane returned to its placid, calm existence but with added dinner parties and visiting between houses. A camaraderie had sprung up between the neighbours, and extended to Claudia, Niamh and Greta. It was a rare week that they all didn't meet up, ignoring the media that descended on them again once the news broke of the widow's arrest. Just like the initial flurry of press and TV after the murder, the journalists soon melted away in search of more lurid stories.

One day in late October, a mild day for the time of year with the golden light of a true Irish autumn spilling through the riot of colourful foliage, three cars pulled up at Eve's house. A group of people spilled out, their laughter and excited chatter alerting everyone to visitors. A tall, broad-shouldered man with a shock of curly dark hair and bright blue eyes called out to Eve as she opened her door.

"Seamus?"

"That's myself," He hugged her without ceremony and pointed to his family. "That's the brood, here. Wee Con, you talked to on the phone." He pointed to a sturdy little toddler who was already making friends with Dymphna, with a child's unerring instinct for a soft touch. "And my wife, Anita and our daughter Molly. And here is my distant cousin Anna O'Reilly and her brother."

More smiles and handshakes and waves as the O'Reilly-Farrell clan introduced themselves in turn. Eve could see quite a resemblance between them all, but it was clear that in temperament this generation took after the nice side of the family, not the avaricious William. "We won't stay," Seamus said. "We've just come from the solicitors and we wanted to share our news with you all. Firstly - thank you so much for recovering Julia's diary, and the jewels. It not only filled in gaps in our family history, but it reunited two sides of a family."

A cheer went up from both his family and the residents of Bramble Lane. "Now, these jewels, they brought a lot of strife over the years. We could fight it out in court, and try to grab a share. As it turns out, they're *fabulously* valuable. But our newly discovered cousins here, they're generous and decent people. They are more interested in having a united family, than feuding. We all had a confab and we thought about it and

- well, the long and the short of it is, we've agreed to sell the jewellery and with the money we're going to set up the Julia O'Reilly Foundation, which will fund a scholarship for young women to attend further education."

A huge cheer, punctuated by whoops and exclamations greeted this announcement.

"Oh!" Eve clapped her hands and joined in the uproar. Tears pricked at her eyes and she had the strangest feeling that Julia Farrell, nee O'Reilly, was right there with them. She had had to escape Kimberly Cottage, but initially she had loved the little house, had met her precious Con because of it and had been saved by the ordinary folk of Bramble Lane. All the good now outweighed the bad, in the end.

"That's perfect, Seamus, just perfect. How proud she would be!" "There are a lot of young ones who need a helping hand," Anna O'Reilly said. "There are girls out there who would make a great fist of things, if someone gave them a chance. Lots of communities, like Traveller women and refugees and immigrants, as well as women who need to work and pass up their chance for their family."

"I know someone who fits that bill," Claudia smiled brightly. "Give me your email and I'll forward on her details. Amanda is her name, very bright girl and she's supporting her mother and sisters..." Anna O'Reilly was putty in the hands of the Brigadier. If Eve had been a betting woman, she'd have put a crisp fifty on Amanda receiving the first scholarship.

Once the O'Reilly-Farrells had taken their leave, pressing invitations on everyone to visit them in Kilkenny and Tipperary, Ronan Desmond called out to the others. "Pop into mine later? Say about eight o'clock?" "I'll bring some buns," Dymphna said. "Claudia, why don't you and Greta stay for dinner? We'll head to Ronan's afterwards."

Niamh joined Eve and Tom in Kimberly Cottage, all three promising to adjourn to Ronan's later. There was no need to ask Margaret whether she was attending; Ronan and she had been inseparable for weeks now. The young teacher had regained her happy -go-lucky nature, especially when she received official word that her role in the O'Reilly affair would not lead to any legal repercussions. She had faced a difficult hour with her Principal, explaining her past and the decisions Brian had forced on her but that woman was an understanding and experienced educator. There was no question of firing a teacher like Margaret. Ronan was like a different man, now that they were officially a couple. Eve thought they were a perfect match, all things considered. Margaret softened Ronan's aloof manner and he bolstered her self-confidence.

She paused on the doorstep and listened. There were still birds in the trees, but the trees were almost fully bare. There was hardly any sound of traffic, and the air was sharp with the slight tang of frost. Eve remembered the day she had moved in, hoping to begin a new life chapter. She had found the fresh start she craved, but it had come rooted in the past, and in traditions she had left behind her. It had brought new people, but also reunited so many old friends and even brought a whole family full circle. It was magic, she thought. Real magic, deep down and in the bones.

Smiling, she patted the front door of her beloved Kimberly and whispered, "Thank you." Then she went inside to her mother and dear friend, and her future.

# Irish Folk Magic

All the traces of Irish folk magic mentioned in The Kimberly Killing are based on authentic Irish folk traditions.

There are many traditional potions used for cures, protection and spells. Claudia Warren has her special potion designed to loosen tongues - this is based on actual potions said to be supplied by Bean Feasa or "Wise women" throughout the last three centuries of recorded folk lore. In the early days of the Irish State, a project called the School's Folklore collection asked school children nationwide to collect folk tales and superstitions from their parents and grandparents. It is available online and is a fascinating insight into Irish cultures. Among these funny, poignant records are countless examples of our shared belief in magic. For example, the following entry records a grandparent's list of herbs and their uses https://www.duchas.ie/en/cbes/4921623/4885877/5153217

Other entries record potions used to make people forget, appear sick, fall in love, and like Claudia's potion, tell the truth!

Hanselling is an ancient tradition, mainly found in Dublin. It's origins lie at least in Middle English and probably in Viking era settlements. In Ireland, it means to give a gift that brings luck, usually to mark new beginnings. My father was said to have the gift of Hanselling new babies. Many people in our neighbourhood of inner city Dublin where he grew up and still worked, brought their babies to him to be hanselled. This involved pressing a coin into the babies hand and would ensure the child would never want. In his youth the tenements and working-class areas of Dublin were among the poorest in Europe and this tradition was taken very seriously indeed. He would also hansel new purses, or wallets, to ensure good luck, and people came to him when changing jobs and starting new enterprises. They also came, too many of them, to be hanselled when emigrating.

Since his death this year, the role has passed to me.

Shape Shifting is a part of Irish mythology and folklore. In the story of **Tuan mac Cairill**, he became over his lifetime a stag, a wild boar, a hawk and finally a salmon prior to being eaten and then reborn as a human. Étain, in the Wooing of Étain, was turned into a fly, swallowed by a Queen, who then gave birth to Étain in human form. In Folklore we have stories of people turning into or being turned into animals e.g. https://www.duc has.ie/en/cbes/4658434/4655180/4659511

Many Wise Women were said to have the "sight." This is a power that can range from seeing the future to an ability to project themselves into the past, to see the truth of a situation. Rather than psychic powers, which come unbidden in flashes or visions, to have the sight implies a degree of control and skill in its use.

The ability to sweet-talk and persuade comes under the Irish word "plámás" pronounced roughly "*plawe-**mawz**.*" This can mean flattery but like many Irish words, defies direct translation into English. It really means an ability to butter up, soften up, convince, flatter, sweet-talk. The Irish "gift of the gab" in short!

I hope you have enjoyed this short explanation of the Irish folk magic mentioned in The Kimberly Killing. All books in this series will come with extras like this, so please do follow me at my newsletter! https://mailchi.mp/c5d9815e1c52/newsletter-signup

I promise not to spam you and to provide some fun Irish news and insights as well as special offers and pre-order prices on books.

# Tea Brack

Tea Brack is one of the most popular goodies in Ireland. This is the recipe I use, it's a common basic recipe for tea brack also known as Barm Brack or Bairín Brack. Bairín is an Irish word which means speckled, referring to the fruit in the mixture.

The cooking time is a bit vague because we tend to add more fruit or more tea erratically so sometimes you need to cook a little longer but an hour is minimum.

I hope you enjoy and if you google, you will find loads of recipes that are variants on this one.


25g/8oz Self-Raising Flour
350g packet Fruit Mix (raisins, sultanas)
300ml/½ pint cold Tea
125g/4oz Golden Caster Sugar or Brown sugar (or half/half)
1 Egg, beaten
One spoon Mixed Spice
One shot of Whiskey (optional)

How to:
Place fruit and tea (and whiskey) in bowl and leave to soak

overnight.

Add sugar, egg, flour and mixed spice.

Mix well. Use a large wooden spoon for preference and keep turning mixture until there are no dry floury patches and it is well combined

Transfer to a greased and base lined 900g/2lb loaf tin or a 20cm/8" round cake tin.

Bake in a preheated oven 170°C/325°F/Gas 3 for 1 hour to 90 minutes * or until risen and firm to the touch.

Cool on a wire tray. When cold wrap in grease-proof paper and keep for two days before cutting.

· The trick is to cover with foil at the one hour mark, then leave for another 30 mints to ensure it's well cooked in the middle but doesn't get overdone on the outside.

# About the Author

N ina Hayes lives in Dublin, Ireland. She is a teacher and writer as well as mother to two lovely boys and wife to a very understanding, long-suffering husband. Her teaching work is centered on Irish folklore, myth and folk magic. All of the magical or folk elements incorporated into her work are based on indigenous Irish traditions and beliefs.

Nina writes from her home in Dublin but loves to travel, around Ireland as well as abroad. She has several hobbies including knitting and paper crafts, gardening and music. At fifty three, she believes in writing books that feature strong female characters of all ages.

If you enjoyed this book, the author is happy to receive feedback from readers at author@ninahayesauthor.com or using the links below.You can also sign up for her newsletter, for special offers, free short stories and more.

http://www.ninahayesauthor.com

https://www.twitter.com/ninahayesauthor

https://www.facebook.com/NinaHayesAuthor

https://www.tiktok.com/@ninahayesauthor

https://mailchi.mp/c5d9815e1c52/newsletter-signup